SUMMER of
adventures

ANN ALMA

PRESS

Winlaw, British Columbia

CONCORDIA
LUTHERAN SCHOOL

Text copyright © 2002 by Ann Alma

Cover illustration © 2002 by Ljuba Levstek

National Library of Canada Cataloguing in Publication Data

Alma, Ann, 1946-
    Summer of adventures / Ann Alma.

    (Summer series ; 2)
    ISBN 1-55039-122-4

    1. Schizophrenia--Juvenile fiction. 2. Family--Juvenile fiction. 3. New Denver
(B.C.)--Juvenile fiction. I. Title. II. Series
PS8551.L565S84 2002   jC813'.54 C2002-911144-7
PZ7.A445Su 2002

Sono Nis Press most gratefully acknowledges the support for our publishing
program provided by the Government of Canada through the Book Publishing
Industry Development Program (BPIDP), The Canada Council for the Arts, and the
British Columbia Arts Council.

Edited by Ann Featherstone, Freda Nobbs and Audrey McLellan
Cover design by Jim Brennan

Published by
SONO NIS PRESS
PO Box 160
Winlaw, BC V0G 2J0
1-800-370-5228
sononis@islandnet.com
www.islandnet.com/sononis/

Distributed in the U.S. by
Orca Book Publishers
Box 468
Custer, WA 98240-0468
1-800-210-5277

Printed and bound in Canada.

Acknowledgements

A big thank you to all the people who helped me to edit this novel, especially the students in Mrs. Lorna Inkster's Gifted and Enrichment Program. They are Oscar, (DESK); Kirra, (Brent Kennedy Elem.); Kaitlin, (Salmo Elem.); Joshua, (Blewett Elem.); Kristina, (Redfish Elem.); Laura, (South Nelson Elem.); Kyle, (Salmo Elem.); Cristina, (Hume Elem.); George, (Hume Elem.); Melinda, (Rosemont Elem.); Celina, (Central Elem.); Caitlin, (A.I. Collinson Elem.). Their hard work and enthusiasm made the group editing experience a pleasure for all. THANKS!

My gratitude also goes to Ann Featherstone, Freda Nobbs and Audrey McClellan for their fine editing.

Thank you to Ruby Truly and the Nikkei Internment Memorial Centre Staff for their suggestions and helpful information. Also for recommending *A Path of Leaves: A Guided Study to the Nikkei Internment Memorial Centre.* (Kyowakai Society, Box 273, New Denver, B.C. V0G 1S0)

Thank you to the women in my writing group, Marylee Banyard, Jennifer Craig and Catharine Mansfield.

I am also grateful for the support I received from the Nelson Conservation Office and the helpful staff at the Nelson Municipal Library.

Author's Note: Because of constant changes in knowledge about mental illnesses, some of the information about schizophrenia may soon be out of date.

To the memories of my dad,
Jacobus Henderikus Alma.

CHAPTER 1

"If you let go I'll drown." Anneke's teeth chattered. She stood up to her waist in a rushing mountain stream, the icy water soaking her clothes. The end of a rope was tied into a loop that she'd slipped over her right wrist. She had worked her way out into the water alongside a huge tree branch that swayed in the stream and was anchored by some boulders. The going had been easy enough while she'd still had a part of the tree beside her. But when she ran out of branch to hold onto, she had stubbornly waded on anyway. She was so close to *the thing*, so close.

"Just one more step. Don't let go."

"I've got the line wrapped around a tree," Ken called. With his feet braced against a large root, his twelve-year-old body anchored the other end of the rope. His face red, he yelled, "Just leave it. It's too dangerous. Get out of the water."

Anneke took another wobbly step. *The thing*, a small, wet, shiny woodcarving that glistened in the sunlight, lay on a shallow gravel bar in the middle of the stream, just out of reach of her left hand. Bending over, she stretched her fingertips towards the object.

"You'd better get out," Ken yelled again.

She reached farther, a bit farther yet, her left arm stretched out, her head bent low. A wave crashed into her ear and she breathed in sharply and shivered, then shook her head impatiently. She was too close to give up now. As she straightened, her bare feet teetered on some slippery rocks before she managed to steady herself. Unlooping the rope from her right arm, she switched it to her left hand. Then, reaching with her right hand, she bent and stretched again. Now her finger-tips touched the red-coloured object. She moved another fraction, then snatched the carving from the gravel, the wet rope slipping from her grasp at the same time.

Anneke's feet slipped, then suddenly went out from under her as she plunged into the creek. While her knee hit something hard, she tried to grab a rock, then a big log. Missing both of them, she floundered down the stream, her head above water, then under. Above again.

As she was swept along helplessly, a plank, stuck between two huge boulders, loomed in front of her. She spread her arms. When her stomach hit the wood, Anneke closed her arms and legs around the plank in a crablike grip. Catching her breath, she looked up at the bank for signs of Ken or her dog, Sheera.

The border collie came rushing up to the edge of the water, ready to jump in for the rescue.

"Get Ken and the rope," Anneke called. "Go fetch."

Sheera took a step into the surging water, backed

up, whined. Then she barked as Ken came running along the bank, dragging the line behind him. The loop, still tied at the end, snagged on a branch, jerking him off his feet. He muttered something under his breath as he hit the ground. Jumping up, he brushed the dirt from his hands before he unhooked the rope.

"Hurry," Anneke shouted. The water tugged at her, pushing her lanky body back and forth on the slippery wood while her long legs, straddling the plank, began hurting, and her hands, gripping together, started slipping. Wild waves washed over her.

"I'll throw you this end," he yelled, trying to swing the rope like a lasso.

"Tie the other end—" She caught a wave full in the face. "—to a tree first," she finished. "And hurry. I'm losing my grip."

He tied the line, then heaved the loop, aiming carefully. Anneke let go with one hand. She stretched towards the flying rope. Grabbed. Missed.

Ken reeled in. Threw again. Again. On the fifth try Anneke clutched the rope. Quickly hooking the loop around her wrist and winding the rope around one arm several times, she let go of the plank.

The line tightened. Ken pulled, the full weight of his chubby body anchoring the rope. Anneke half swam, half stumbled on the rocky creek bottom as she reeled herself in. Her feet slipped. She kicked the water with a swimming motion. Skinned her knee. Banged her elbow. Found her footing again. Walked two steps. Fell again on her already sore knee. Ken hauled and heaved until Anneke's hands caught hold of a tree root sticking out of the bank. She clambered onto the bank, stood up and scrambled out. Sheera whined and licked her dripping hands, sniffed and licked her scraped knee.

"Thanks." Unwinding the rope from her arm, Anneke rubbed the red marks it left, while Ken brushed dirt off his shorts and shirt. He looked at his dirty shoes. "Oh well," he shrugged.

Anneke reached into her shorts pocket and held the carving up triumphantly.

"You're crazy!" Ken's brown eyes filled with awe and surprise.

She shrugged her bony shoulders. "I said I'd get it." She rubbed water from her eyes with her other hand.

"Yeah, but..." He took the carving she held out to him.

"Well," she prompted.

"Well what?"

"Is it like the other carvings your mom has? You're the one who saw this thing on that gravel bar. And *you* said it looked just like one of your mom's Japanese carvings."

Ken turned the object in his hand. Slowly his face lit up as he said, "I think it might be. My mom will love to see this."

"I wish I'd worn my bathing suit." Anneke raked her fingers through her short brown hair and shivered in spite of the midsummer heat. She'd been busy showing off to Ken, walking into the creek after he'd spotted the object on the gravel bar, doing what she'd said she would do. She had forgotten how cold these West Kootenay mountain streams were, how they came from melting glacial ice.

Ken was still studying the carving. He nodded slowly, scratching his head under his brush cut, then mumbled something.

"What?" Anneke said, getting more excited. She could see by the concentration on her friend's face that this carving was important to him. And if it was, it had to be valuable. Ken knew a lot about these kinds of things. He was always reading books.

"I think this could be an antique," he said, polishing the object on his shirt.

It *had* to be. Ken never used his clothes to clean something. But now he studied the carving some more, slowly turning it to view all sides and holding it up close to see the finer details.

Anneke shivered again. "I'm going to change out of these wet clothes," she said, walking back to where she had left her bag.

Ken followed with the rope and the carving. "Let's have lunch," he said.

"I see you're back to thinking about your favourite subject, food," she teased him. "Well, I'm changing into my dry bathing suit first." She went behind a thick shrub.

After Anneke's dripping clothes were spread over some bushes in the sun, the two friends ate their peanut butter-and-banana sandwiches. Sheera ate her dog biscuit before finding a stick to chew on.

"Let me have a good look." Anneke studied the carving, which just fit into the palm of her hand. When she looked closely, she saw the figure was a little man with a fat belly and a sack flung over his shoulder. "It's beautifully carved," she said with admiration. "Very delicate work. Whoever made this was an expert carver. I wish I was this good. I'm surprised this little guy isn't chipped from the gravel and the wild water."

"This kind of wood is really hard," Ken said, his mouth full. "I really do think it's an old Japanese antique made of mahogany wood."

"Would your mom know for sure?" Anneke shivered. Goosebumps still showed on her arms and legs.

Ken shrugged. "My mom has four of these kinds of carvings. They came from Japan, a long, long time ago. They're good luck gods. Obasan, that's my grandmother, brought them with her from Vancouver when her family was forced to move during the Second World War. When Obasan died, my mom got them. They're part of a set of seven good luck gods. The other three are missing."

"Could this be one of the missing ones?" Anneke asked hopefully.

"Maybe. Mom sometimes looks in antique stores to see if she can find those other three gods, but the ones she finds are always just a bit different or not the right kind of wood. They're not part of her set."

Anneke stroked the carving. "So this *could* be one of them?" Forgotten were the dripping clothes on the bushes, the goosebumps on her bare arms.

"Yeah, maybe. That would be so cool. Let's show Mom. She'll know. And if she's not totally sure she can probably ask at the Nikkei Internment Memorial Centre at New Denver."

"Where?" Anneke raised her eyebrows.

"The Nikkei Centre. It's a place where Canadians who came from Japan many years ago, like my grandparents, were forced to live during the Second World War. I've been there."

"Oh right, I think I've heard of it," Anneke said vaguely. She brightened. "New Denver has this great store where you can get yummy ice cream. It's the best. And there's really good hiking trails and beaches and—"

"Hey," Ken broke in. "If you showed her the carving, maybe Mom would take both of us to the centre to check it out. Then, after, we could do some of that stuff."

"Yeah," Anneke said excitedly. "Like camping at Rosebery." When Ken looked questioningly, she added, "Just north of New Denver. There's a campground right by a river."

"We've never gone camping. But Darryl—you know, Mom's new boyfriend..." Ken rolled his eyes and sighed before his face brightened again. "He likes to camp. I heard him talking to my mom about it. He was trying to convince her to go. If I'm on his side, maybe Mom will give in. It'd be a real adventure. I'd like to see my mom sleep in a tent, on the ground!"

"Or you," Anneke grinned. "Your clothes might get dirty! You work on the boyfriend, and I'll give this to your mom."

"Don't say anything to her about the camping until after I talk to Darryl," Ken advised.

"Fine. But do it soon. I haven't done anything exciting for weeks. I'm tired of plain old walks with Sheera or just riding my bike down the road. And I'm just about going crazy with boredom."

CHAPTER 2

Mrs. Uno, Ken's mom, was more than excited about the carving; she was ecstatic. The little man was made of the same kind of red hardwood as the rest of her set. She told them it was a netsuke, a Japanese piece of art, probably carved many, many years ago. Mrs. Uno unlocked and opened the glass doors on one of the cabinets in her living room to show Anneke the four netsuke she owned.

"This is Ebisu," she explained. "The god of the fisherman." The little red man held a fish and a rod.

Anneke admired the way the artist had carved the details on the face of the god and on the body of the fish. "I wish I could carve like that," she said.

"This is Benten," Mrs. Uno continued, handing Anneke a little goddess with eight arms who was riding a dragon. "She is the goddess of art, luck, and wisdom."

Anneke loved the goddess of art right away. "I'll swap you for the one I found," she offered.

But Mrs. Uno shook her head. "It's a family treasure," she explained. She went on to show the two remaining gods, Bishamon, the warrior, and Jurojin, the god of happiness in old age.

Next Mrs. Uno opened a book about Japanese art treasures, pointing with a long painted fingernail to a picture of the netsuke Anneke had found. He was Hotei, the god of wealth and happiness. If this netsuke was part of her set, she told Anneke, she would love to buy it from her. Especially since, if it *did* turn out to be part of this set of seven gods, Hotei might once have belonged to a distant relative.

Mrs. Uno played with her gold ring absent-mindedly before she picked Hotei up and held it out to Anneke. Then she hesitated. "Make *sure* you give this to one of your foster parents right away, as *soon* as you get home," she said, not quite wanting to let Hotei go. "Or maybe you could leave the netsuke here for now, with these others?"

But Anneke, feeling important, shook her head, put Hotei in her hiking shorts pocket, and buttoned the pocket shut.

Mrs. Uno locked the cabinet doors before she said, "I'd love to take you both to New Denver. I'll buy you a treat and take you to the Nikkei Centre. Be sure and bring the netsuke, Anneke. Would your family like to come?" She carefully rearranged a short strand of jet-black hair on her forehead.

"I'll ask," Anneke promised. "Larry probably has to work. Otherwise he might. He loves outings."

She didn't tell Mrs. Uno that Eileen loved antiques. She also decided not to tell Larry and Eileen about the netsuke for now. She was the one who had rescued the carving in the first place, and she was quite capable of looking after it. Why should she give her treasure to her foster parents?

When she got home, she found Eileen, her foster mom, in the garden.

"Hi," Anneke said, leaning her bike against the shed. "Guess what. Mrs. Uno is taking us to New Denver next Saturday. If you really, really want to come, I'm sure you could try to get invited too."

"That's OK," Eileen said, taking off one garden glove and pushed back the long brown hair that was sticking to her sweaty forehead. "Phew, it's hot out here." She grabbed her water bottle and drank deeply before she continued. "Larry has to work, and Elishia and I need to bake a cake. We're helping out at the preschool bake sale on Saturday afternoon.

"Oh well," Anneke shrugged. "Too bad." But she was glad they were busy. It would be more fun without Eileen. And four-year-old Elishia always wanted so much attention.

"But you go," Eileen said. "It sounds exciting."

"It *might* turn into a camping trip," Anneke added.

Eileen frowned. "Oh, in that case I'd better talk to Larry."

Anneke sighed. Did that mean Eileen wouldn't

let her go if they went camping? Calling Sheera, she grumbled, "I'm going to my workshop."

With the dog in tow, she walked down the path at the end of the large country garden. The workshop, partly hidden behind a hedge, was a private space where Anneke did her own carving and carpentry projects. She took a key ring from her belt and unlocked the padlock on the door. Pushing it open, she stood at the threshold for a moment, taking in the brightness of the sunlight streaming through the windows. Dust particles danced over the table and chairs, the workbench with tools, the shelves of carvings, and the chunks of wood. Tenderly Anneke took the little carving of the Japanese god from her pocket and placed it on a shelf beside some of her own pieces. For now this little treasure would fit here perfectly, in this special place, in Anneke's own world.

Imagine if Ken did manage to get his mom excited about going camping and then she, Anneke, the outdoors expert and camping guru, couldn't go! How frustrating that would be. She shrugged her shoulders and decided to pin her hopes on Larry. He would let her go.

Rummaging through the wood chips on the bench, she found the figure of a sitting dog she'd whittled for Mr. Martin, a friend of Larry. She'd take the carving to Mr. Martin's house now and get paid the promised $7.50. And if Mrs. Uno did buy this Japanese carving, she'd use that money as well to buy a bunch of CDs. This place needed some different music. Since she'd moved back to this foster home, about a year ago, she'd only had two CDs. The one she'd bought with her own money she played all the time. The other, the one Eileen had given her, the one with soppy, country-and-western songs, lay on the shelf under a thick layer of dust. She should clean it off and give it to Elishia. No. Elishia had enough CDs. Eileen bought her two last month for her birthday. Two CDs with little kids' songs everyone had to sing along with. Eileen thought that was great, but it was enough to drive any twelve-year-old crazy. Elishia certainly would not get this CD. Maybe Mother would like to have it at her group home. Maybe, wrapped up, this CD would make a nice present for Mother during the picnic tomorrow. No, Eileen would be there. Some other time then, during another of Anneke's once-a-week outings with Mother, she would give her the CD.

Opening a cooler that stood in one corner, Anneke took out a slice of cheese. Breaking it in half, she called, "Here, Sheera," and gave her a piece. Carrying her own half outside, she went to her bicycle.

As Anneke was about to pedal away, Eileen opened the front door, a big pink hair clip in one hand. "Where are you and Sheera off to?"

"I'm delivering a carving."

"Remember, you need to check these things with me." Eileen put the hair clip in her mouth while gathering her long, unruly hair up from her shoulders with both hands and twisting it into a bird's nest on her head.

"If this place is a prison then why don't you put up a high fence," Anneke mumbled.

But Eileen had heard her. Taking the clip from her mouth, she said, "Just a minute, young lady. That was very rude. It's certainly not the way to get permission to go camping." She imprisoned her wild hair with the hair clip. *Snap.* The whole contraption was caught on the top of her head.

"I said we *might* go camping. I don't know yet." Anneke rolled her blue eyes upward in a gesture of hopelessness and started biking down the driveway. But she didn't get far.

"You haven't told me where you are going," Eileen called. "Besides, with that attitude you'd better stay home right now."

"Home?" Anneke yelled. "Oh, you mean this place." She threw her bike on the ground in the middle of the driveway and started marching defiantly back to the workshop. But then she stopped herself. She really did want to go to New Denver, and Eileen could spoil things. She'd whine about Anneke's attitude to Larry as soon as he got home. Anneke sighed.

"Sorry," she mumbled, picking up her bike and leaning it against the side of the house. She called Sheera and went back to her workshop. Why couldn't she live only with Larry until Mother was better? Her foster dad was an easy enough guy to get along with. But her foster mother was too nosy and treated her too much like Elishia. Didn't Eileen realize there was a huge difference between being four years old and being twelve?

Frustrated, she grabbed a broom from a corner of the workshop and started sweeping the bench and the floor. She took the wood chips to the firewood bin. Then she pulled her camping foamy and sleeping bag from the bottom shelf and sat on them. Taking a new chunk of wood, she mumbled, "What should I carve this time?" Sheera, who had sat down beside her on the floor, wagged her tail. Turning the piece of wood slowly in her hands, studying it from all sides, Anneke said, "You want me to carve another dog, I bet. But I've already made too many that look like you." Sheera, ears up, head turned to one side for better understanding, gazed unblinkingly at her with piercing brown eyes. Anneke stroked the animal's soft black-and-white head. "Maybe a duck? Or another fish?" She'd mostly carved animal figures, she suddenly realized. That's who she was: Anneke, the woodworker, the animal carver. Maybe some day she'd be a famous Canadian carver. Her art would be worth a lot of money. Photos of her carvings would be shown in expensive, heavy books like the ones Mrs. Uno bought and put on her coffee table. Her artwork would be locked away behind glass doors.

Studying the block of wood some more, holding it this way and that, she settled on a squirrel. After getting some nature books from the living room bookshelves and looking closely at photos and sketches of squirrels, Anneke took out her new tools. Instead of using the Swiss Army knife that always hung from the key ring on her belt, she now used a real set of carving tools. And a vise on the workbench, to clamp the wood into. Starting with the bushy tail curled up over the squirrel's back, she set to work.

To make the rough outline of the tail, she used the larger chisel first. The edge was sharp, but the wood was hard. Anneke used her hammer to tap the chisel down through a knot in the wood. She took the smaller chisel and scraped it over the carved part, then pushed with all her strength when she got to the knot. The chisel slipped and nicked her finger.

"Ouch!" Anneke dropped the tool. She looked at the blood that bubbled out of the cut and started running down her finger. Quickly she put the bleeding finger in her mouth while with her other hand she took a bandage from an open box on the shelf. Annoyed with her clumsiness, she struggled to get the bandage open and ready to stick over the cut. Eileen would ask why she had yet another bandaged finger. Larry, even though he had given her these bandages for her workshop, would frown. He would question again if the new tools were too sharp for her, if she were careful enough.

But the tools were fine, Anneke thought. And she knew how to use them properly. Getting cut from time to time was just part of being a wood-worker. And even though she almost always had at least one little bandage on one of her fingers, and the cuts were sometimes annoying or even painful, she usually forgot about them soon. Working with gloves on, as Larry had suggested, was just too cumbersome.

Anneke took her finger out of her mouth, quickly wiped it dry on her T-shirt, and wrapped the bandage around the cut tightly before the newly formed red drops could start to run down her finger.

Returning to her project, she continued carving. Soon the outline of a squirrel's bushy tail started to show.

By the time she went in to supper, Anneke was in a better mood. Larry was home. Cornering him in the living room alone, her hands in her pockets, Anneke asked if she could go camping with the Unos *if* they went to Rosebery on the weekend.

"Mrs. Uno is into *camping?*" Larry asked, his eyebrows shooting up.

"No, not really, but she has a new boyfriend who is. And I could help to teach her and Ken how to camp without getting too dirty."

Larry laughed out loud. "You! Teach someone how to stay clean in the outdoors? Now I've heard it all."

"Well, I could do the dirty jobs, chopping wood and looking after the fire so they can stay clean," she grinned.

"If you do get invited, I'll have to talk to Mrs. Uno first," Larry said. "I'd come myself, but I'll be working."

"Can I sleep out in the workshop tonight?" Anneke asked. "I haven't done much camping this summer."

"Sure. You can sharpen up your skills in there."

Even though Anneke loved her bedroom full of colourful pictures and a soft bed, she loved hanging out in her workshop more. Elishia, already in her pyjamas, came in for a while to play Pick-up Sticks. Anneke let the little girl win the first, but not the second game. Then she gave her a big, snuggly hug and said, "Eight o'clock. To bed, to bed, Miss Pumpkinhead," and chased her out, pretending to be a big, fierce animal.

Elishia squealed as she ran barefoot up the path. But then she turned and came back.

"I want to play more," she begged, throwing her arms around Anneke's neck and kissing her forehead.

"No, we were supposed to play only one game and we already snuck in a second one." Anneke firmly blocked Elishia's attempt to get back into the workshop. She loved her little foster sister, but sometimes Elishia could be a pest. She always wanted more attention than Anneke was ready to give.

"I have to—" Elishia started.

But Anneke quickly interrupted with, "Remember, you need to check if the little seeds you planted still have enough water."

"Ohhh," Elishia exclaimed, clasping her hand over her mouth. "My poppy seeds." She hurried out and Anneke quickly closed the door behind her.

She took Sheera for a long walk in the warm summer evening, the way she and Mother used to do before Mother went back to the hospital last year. The way she and Larry did some evenings when they wanted to talk about some of their favourite things: camping, hiking, wildlife, woodworking, how Mother was doing lately.

Making sure Eileen didn't see them leave, Anneke and Sheera snuck down the long driveway. Larry always agreed that Anneke could walk her dog alone in the evenings, but Eileen usually argued with him about dangers. As if there was anything that could hurt Anneke on these quiet Slocan Valley country roads. As if Sheera wouldn't be there to protect her anyway.

After a while the last of the daylight faded and the moon began to outline the mountains on either side of the narrow valley. Stars started twinkling high above. Anneke and Sheera loved to wander the lonely roads that divided the valley's properties. The dog ran ahead, sniffing for trails in the roadside weeds and scaring small wild animals.

A neighbour's two horses came lumbering over, creating little dust clouds with each step. They leaned their heads across the fence and wanted to be scratched behind the ears. Reaching up, Anneke deeply inhaled the strong, sweet, animal smells.

A little later a coyote howled in the far distance. Sheera barked. Anneke calmed the alert dog with a whispered "Shh, shhh." The coyote howled twice more. Once another neighbour drove by with a little honked greeting and a wave. Then for a while all was so still they could almost hear the moon shining.

Just after ten o'clock Anneke was back in her workshop. She took Sheera's brush and stroked it gently through her pet's long soft hair. When Anneke rubbed the dog's belly, Sheera sighed. From time to time she gave little doggie groans of pleasure.

Anneke drank a small carton of cold milk she'd kept in the cooler in her workshop, ate two cookies, and fed Sheera her bedtime dog biscuit. After going up to the house to brush her teeth and swap her workshop cooler's used ice pack for a colder one, she stuck her head around the living room door and said goodnight.

Lying in her sleeping bag on her foamy on the wooden floor, Anneke thought about Rosebery. She hoped they would go; she loved sleeping in a tent. Sheera would be on her own blanket beside her, the way she was now. Then Anneke's thoughts wandered to the place they often went, to her real mother.

She got up, found a small leather wallet that hung from the belt on her hiking shorts and opened it to her mother's pictures. One was of Anneke as a baby in Mother's arms. One was of Mother taken a few weeks ago. She was sitting on the bench at the park, looking over her shoulder at the camera, a smile on her face. "Get better soon, Mama," Anneke whispered. She snapped the wallet shut and crawled back into her sleeping bag.

Tomorrow Anneke, Mother, Larry, Eileen and Elishia were all going to a small lake for a picnic.

Ken had wanted to come, but Mother's doctor had said no, this was a big enough group for Mother already. Anneke had been relieved to hear this. Ken had never met her real mother, and Anneke wasn't sure she wanted him to meet her now. Doctor Sunnybrook didn't really want Sheera to go either. But Anneke had insisted, saying, "Sheera goes where I go. Mother likes her."

Even though Mother was doing much better with the help of new medication, her schizophrenia was not really under control yet. Little trips still needed to be calm and uneventful. Anneke hoped the illness would soon be manageable, as the doctor kept promising it might be. Then maybe Mother could move out of the group home, rent a place, and the two of them, and Sheera, could live together again as a family. Of course Anneke would miss Larry a lot. But she could still visit here.

She yawned and snuggled deeper into her warm sleeping bag. She and Mother would have fun, playing games, watching TV, having picnics all the time. Mother didn't treat Anneke like a little kid. Even when the two of them and Sheera still lived together, before Mother was put in a hospital, when Anneke was only nine and ten and eleven years old, Mother had often let her be in charge. Of course Anneke was littler then and had actually needed Mother to be more of a *real* mother. But now she was a whole year older. And Mother *would* be better soon. Anneke was sure of that.

CHAPTER 3

Come on, Elishia." Impatiently Anneke opened the car door. "It's time to visit my mother. Get in."

Eileen buckled her daughter into the car seat while Anneke held the other door open for Sheera. Then she crawled in beside her dog and the little girl.

"I hope Elishia won't get too active for your mom," Eileen said, a worried look on her face. "Maybe we should take some toys to keep her busy while—"

"We'll be fine," Larry said as he started the car. "Nature will provide all the toys we need."

Anneke sighed contentedly. They were off. Larry really liked Mother. He worked at an adult group home, so he always knew exactly what to say or do when Mother acted or talked differently. And Eileen was wrong: Mother would be fine with Elishia. When Anneke was a little four-year-old herself, Mother had loved to play with her. But that was before her schizophrenia had started.

Eileen began singing Elishia's favourite song, "Banana Phone" and soon everyone chimed in, acting silly and screeching out the words "Ring, ring, ring, ring." After a while they stopped at one of their favourite spots to look at the trees and the river flashing by.

"Let's get out for a minute," Larry said.

"What time is it?" Anneke asked.

"We're a bit early actually," Larry said. "You always chase us out of the house too soon when we go to see your mom."

Everyone walked to the river, and Sheera jumped in for a swim before anyone could stop her.

"We want to tell you girls something," Eileen said, sitting down on a big rock and smoothing her flowered skirt over her knees. Then she jumped up and brushed two ants from her foot.

Larry smiled broadly. "How would you feel about having a new brother or sister?"

Anneke's head swiveled around so quickly her sunglasses shifted on her nose. "You're getting another foster kid?"

"No," Larry beamed. "We are having another baby. Eileen is pregnant."

Anneke's mouth dropped open. She stared at Larry, then quickly glanced at Eileen's stomach, but saw nothing unusual. She stared at Larry again. He looked so happy.

"A baby?" Elishia squealed. "Can I hold her?"

"Yes," Eileen said. "You'll be my big helper."

"I can put on a real diaper, like I do with my

dolly," Elishia said importantly, looking from one face to the next. "I can let the baby watch me comb my dolly's hair."

A butterfly landed on Eileen's bright skirt.

"Oh, a flutter," Elishia said, trying to catch it. When she ran off after the butterfly, Eileen followed.

Larry said, "We wanted you to be one of the first to know."

"Why?" Did this mean they'd ask Anneke to leave? She couldn't live with Mother yet. They knew that. So where could she go? "Where are you sending me?" she asked lamely.

"Sending you? Oh no, you misunderstood." Larry shook his head. "We want you to know because our family is getting bigger. You're part of that. You'll have a new baby brother or sister."

"Foster brother or sister."

"Theoretically, yes. But I hope you know that we feel that you are family. And that this baby will be a real brother or sister to you."

In the silence between her and Larry, Anneke heard Elishia start to talk about Mandy's baby brother. Mandy was Elishia's playschool friend. The brother was a cute, roly-poly baby. But he was also a baby who cried a lot and who needed even more attention than Elishia did. Eileen would be really busy with the new baby. Elishia might get as whiny as Mandy. Anneke sighed. That's all she needed. She'd become nothing but a babysitter then. She looked at Elishia, who stood by the car, holding Eileen's hand. She saw Eileen reaching into the car for Elishia's doll. Anneke felt glad Mother never had another baby. At least she never needed to share Mother when she was little. Or maybe—if she *had* had a real brother or sister, then...Well, she didn't, and that was all there was to it. And now they were going for a picnic with Mother. "We don't want to be late," she said.

Larry playfully punched her shoulder. "We like your mom too, you know. She's a part of our lives." He looked at her carefully for a moment. "OK, we'd better get going."

As they drove on a new section of road, built after a mudslide had washed a section of the old road away, Elishia asked, "Are we there yet?"

"Almost," Larry said.

"I hope Mother's new medication has started working better," Anneke mumbled.

"Wait till you see what's for lunch," Eileen said. "Larry has outdone himself. And I wasn't even allowed to help."

"I'm hungry," Elishia chimed in. "I want some lunch."

"Soon," Larry said as they pulled up in front of the group home.

Quickly Anneke jumped out. "I'll be right back." She let Sheera in the front, to sit at Eileen's feet, and shut the car door.

The front door opened and there stood Mother, her long red hair held off her face with two green clips. She wore jeans and a yellow shirt with green and purple leaves and flowers.

"Hi, Mama," Anneke said, putting her arms around her mother's bony shoulders. "They took you shopping for new clothes. You look nice."

"Hi, Kindeke," Mother said groggily. She hugged her daughter weakly before she picked a bag off the floor. "The cookies," she mumbled.

A caregiver walked over. "Your mom is a bit sleepy today," she said. "It's the new medication. She may nap from time to time. But she made the cookies by herself, didn't you?" She looked at Mother. "Have fun."

Anneke took Mother's hand in hers, carefully carried the cookies in her other hand, and said, "We will. See you later."

At the lake Eileen spread a blanket in the shade of a big tree. Larry had brought two plates of fancy little sandwiches and different kinds of pickled vegetables he'd learned to make at a Doukhobor cooking class.

Everyone sat around the edges of the blanket: Anneke beside Mother, and Larry with Elishia snuggled on his lap. When Eileen, sitting down between Mother and Larry, said, "Isn't this a wonderful picnic?" and touched Mother's arm lightly, Mother shrank back. Anneke glanced at Larry, but he was busy handing Elishia a sandwich. Mother didn't like to be touched by others. Only by Anneke. And then only sometimes. "You sit here," she said, moving Mother over and sitting between her and Eileen. Anneke held her mother's hand, which trembled slightly. With her other hand she moved one of the two plates of sandwiches closer. Larry broke the silence by starting a story about Grubby Graeme, an old prospector who used to live in the Slocan Valley.

"Grubby Graeme never cut his hair," he began, rubbing his own shaven chin. "After years of not using a comb, his beard was so tangled it looked like a bird's nest. Some straw was stuck in it. Bits of sawdust too. Even some pine needles."

Elishia giggled. "Needles?" she said, her mouth full of carrot.

"From a pine tree," Larry said. "See, like these." He showed her some on the ground. "Anyway," he continued, "one night something woke Grubby Graeme from a deep, deep sleep. At first he thought it was water dripping on him from the roof rafters. The weather was terrible: rain, thunder, lightning flashing outside the one small, cobwebbed window. Because of his heavy beard, Grubby Graeme always had to sleep on his back. So he couldn't turn over on his side to snuggle deeper under his two moth-eaten blankets. But, after listening to the weather for a while, he did go back to sleep.

"Soon he woke up again. Something moved across his cheek. Then his forehead."

Elishia swallowed her mouthful of sandwich. Her eyes turned big and round. "Oooooh," she whispered.

Eileen passed her food plate. Larry took another sandwich, removed the sprig of parsley from the top, and gave it to Eileen, who ate it.

Mother, who had only eaten one fancy sandwich

and one pickled bean, yawned so widely her jaw gave a little cracking sound. Anneke smiled at her.

"So," Larry continued, "Grubby Graeme sat up carefully and felt around in the dark for matches. He lit the candle beside his bed. He looked at the flickering light and the dark shapes dancing in the wind blowing through the cracks in the walls. Water dripped into tin cans crowding the dirt floor of the tiny cabin. Water dropped into his one and only cooking pot. It plinked into his tin cup and plonked onto his enamel plate. Drip, drip, drip the rain splattered from the leaky roof. The can right beside his pillow was almost full to overflowing."

"His bed will get wet," Elishia interrupted, her eyes even bigger.

Mother yawned again. She leaned against Anneke, who put her arm around Mother's shoulder. Larry winked at her. Anneke felt a warm tingling all over. This was like a real family. Would adding a baby change that? Would Anneke have to share her room with Elishia? No way. She'd rather move into her workshop. If the baby were a boy, would he and Larry be together all the time, the way Eileen and Elishia were together? Biting into her fourth small sandwich, Anneke looked around the happy circle and noticed that Mother had closed her eyes.

Larry continued his story. "Before Grubby Graeme could make a move to empty the can of water by his pillow, he felt something on his face again. 'What the dickens?' he said."

Elishia, who had put her thumb in her mouth,

pulled it out with a pop and asked, "Was the bed wet?"

"A little bit, yes," Larry said, his eyes twinkling.

Elishia breathed in sharply. She put her hand in front of her mouth and giggled, looking at Larry, then at Anneke, then at Eileen. "The bed is wet," she whispered.

Everyone nodded. They smiled at each other.

Eileen held Mother's bag of cookies out to everyone. "These are lovely," she said. "Your mom did a wonderful job on the red and blue decorations on the cookies."

Anneke took three cookies. Elishia followed her example. Eileen, frowning, was about to say something, but before she could, Larry went on.

"There, in the dim, dancing candlelight, on that bad, blustery night in the wild, wild woods of the Slocan Valley, Grubby Graeme sat in wonder. Because in his long tangly beard, unruly like the brambles growing around the cabin, was a nest. A little nest full of tiny wriggling bodies. A nest with five baby chipmunks. 'Well, I'll be...' Grubby Graeme said."

"How big, Daddy, how big?" Elishia squealed.

"This tiny." Larry made the tip of Elishia's baby finger peek out from between his own big thumb and finger.

Elishia snuggled back against his chest. Mother's head had sank a little lower against Anneke's side. Mother was getting heavy. Anneke didn't move.

"So," Larry went on, "the old prospector took his

32

sharp knife. He carefully sharpened the blade even more on a whetstone and gently, ever so gently, cut the beard off his chin. Cut the beard he had grown all his adult life. He laid the hair nest on the table and took two biscuits. One he crumbled into the nest to feed the mother of his new family. The other one he ate himself to celebrate the new arrivals. From that night on he called his cabin 'The World of Weird Wonders' and he lived happily ever after."

"Oh, Daddy," Elishia said, her brown eyes shining. "Is that a make-believe story?"

"Of course not. It's a make-bologna story," Eileen said. "That's your dad's specialty. He's full of bologna."

Larry tickled Elishia and she jumped off his lap. "I want to swim." She pulled at Anneke's sleeve.

Carefully Anneke slid her sleeping mother away from her shoulder and down onto the blanket that Eileen was smoothing out for her. Anneke wanted to go for a swim too. But could she leave Mother with Eileen? Sure, Larry was here. Besides, Mother was fast asleep and wouldn't miss Anneke if she went for a quick dip. "Sheera, come," she whispered. The dog needed no encouragement.

Eileen took her sandals off and also came to the shallow end of the lake. Standing in deeper water, Anneke looked at the two adults left under the tree. Mother and Larry. Happily she did a duck dive and swam under water as far as she could before romping with Sheera.

All too soon it was time to return Mother to the

group home. While dropping her off, everyone made plans for the next visit.

"How about a hike?" Anneke suggested.

"Not too far. Not yet," the caregiver said. "Your mother's new medication makes her tired and groggy. A board game or a picnic would be better. Something kind of quiet and easy."

"A game of crib and a corn barbecue?" Anneke tried.

"Yes," Mother stated in a loud voice, as if she'd suddenly woken up with a start. "*I want corn!* I love corn. We *never* get corn here." Pulling away the two green clips, she let her long red hair fall across her face. Then she wandered over to a cabinet, took a crib game out of a drawer, slammed the wooden board down on the table, and put the pegs into the holes.

"You had corn yesterday, remember?" the caregiver said.

When Mother ignored everyone and started shuffling a deck of cards, dropping half of them on the floor, Anneke's heart sank. The floaty, bubbly feeling fled. When she felt Larry's hand on her shoulder, she turned towards him. He looked disappointed too.

"How about a barbecue and a game of crib for you, your mom, Gram, and Grump?" he said quietly. "At their place."

"Yes." Anneke knew her foster-grandparents liked Mother. And they loved to play crib. "See you next week." She hugged Mother. "Maybe you could make some more of those delicious cookies," she said. "They were so great."

But Mother started counting out cards on the table. "Goodbye," she mumbled.

Anneke glanced at Eileen, who looked sad. Instead of taking Elishia's outstretched hand, she came over and hugged Anneke, wrapping her completely into her arms for a few seconds. For once, Anneke didn't pull away. She sank slightly into the warmth of Eileen's arms. When they walked outside, Larry put his arm around her shoulder.

For some strange reason, she didn't know why, Anneke suddenly noticed that she and Larry were wearing their exact same hiking shorts, the shorts they'd bought together on their trip to the East Kootenays, on that special Fathers and Daughters hike they had participated in a few weeks ago. Like her, he even wore his brown belt through the loops. She focused on the two belts, almost at the same height. Larry had long legs; his belt was still a bit higher than hers. Not for long though, Anneke decided. She'd shoot past him some day soon.

They walked without talking, his arm around her shoulder, until they reached the car.

CHAPTER 4

The next day, just as Anneke and Eileen came back from dropping Elishia off at Gram and Grump's, Ken phoned. He told Anneke that his mom and Darryl would take them camping on Saturday. "We went into Nelson to buy everything," he said excitedly. "New tents, sleeping bags, air mattresses, and pumps—'the whole nine yards,' as Darryl says."

Anneke went to the kitchen to ask Larry and Eileen for permission. But they had something else on their minds. Larry said, "We want to talk to you."

"Me?" Anneke's first thought was What did I do wrong now? Then another thought hit her. They want me to leave. She sat down at the table, Sheera at her feet.

"There's a reason we took Elishia to Gram's," Eileen said. She put her hand on Larry's.

Anneke's stomach tightened.

"We've been thinking," Larry said. He smiled at Anneke, then at Eileen. "Sometimes we feel that

36

you're not sure if you belong here. So we wondered, would you feel more sure about us as a family if we adopt you."

"Adopt? You mean...What do you mean?"

"If we adopt you," Larry explained, "you would be part of our family forever. You would always be our oldest child. This new baby would be your real brother or sister. I would be your dad and Eileen would be your mom."

"I have a mother." A picture of Mother flashed before Anneke's eyes: Mother as she used to be when Anneke was little. When she called Anneke *Kindeke*, little child. When she played games with Anneke and read her stories and took her to the river for picnics and ice cream. When they snuggled on the couch together and watched game shows, or sang along loudly with silly songs on a tape.

"Eileen can't be my mother," Anneke said, looking only at Larry.

"We know you have your own mom," Larry said. "Of course that won't ever change. You know we all like her very much and care about her deeply."

That was true: Larry, Eileen, Gram, Grump, everyone liked Mother. "Gram and Grump would be my real grandparents," she said.

"Yes, it was actually Grump who first suggested we check out the adoption route," Eileen said. "So you would feel more a part of us all. We've thought about adoption and talked about adoption all week now. Especially since we told you that I am pregnant. And it looks like we *can* adopt you if your mother agrees."

"You never even asked *me?*" Furiously, Anneke looked from one adult to the other. "What am I—a carving that you can trade back and forth?" She jumped up and started for the door, but Larry's voice stopped her.

"Anneke sit down. Maybe we didn't explain all this right. We wanted to check into things first exactly because we didn't want to hurt you. What if we talked to you about the idea first and you said yes and then the adoption authorities told us it couldn't be done?"

When Anneke sat down again, Eileen leaned closer and said, "Your happiness is the most important thing for us here. We all love you. That means we want what's best for you." She smiled at Anneke. "I should tell you two what happened at the beach this morning. Elishia hit Mandy over the head with her plastic shovel. She was angry and upset because Mandy said you weren't her real sister. Elishia loves you. She adores you."

"I know." Anneke got up again. She walked to the door. Stopped. Turned back to look at her foster parents. "I want to think." She opened the door, but didn't leave. When Larry stood up, she noticed that he was wearing his hiking shorts again. She was too.

"Would you like to go for a walk?" he asked.

"Yes...no." Anneke looked at the shorts, the brown belt, the Swiss Army knife that Larry, like her, always wore on the belt ring. "Yes," she said again, knowing that he was already like a real dad anyway. That he would listen if she wanted to talk. Or that they could walk quietly without talking.

Eileen smiled.

She would be my mother, Anneke thought...I *have* a mother!

"No," Anneke said, loudly, with great certainty.

Larry walked closer while Anneke still stood in the open doorway. Mother is doing better, she thought. Eileen says she loves me, but—I know Mama loves me. She always does, even when she is sick. A picture of Mother flashed through her mind again, Mother with her hair hanging wildly across her face, with her shaking hands dropping playing cards all over the floor. Mother is not doing better yet.

Eileen loved Elishia the way Mother loved Anneke. Could Eileen love Anneke that way? Did she? Anneke shook her head. She didn't *want* Eileen to love her that way. Then Mother would have nobody. She would be alone even when she did get better. "No!" she said again, walking out the door.

"Think about it," Larry said, following her out. "There's no need to decide right away. Talk to Sheera. Whatever we decide, this is your home. You will always be a part of our family."

Part of *our* family. How could she be adopted and have two mothers? And what if Eileen had a baby boy and Larry was crazy about him?

Ignoring Larry, who stood on the deck, watching her, Anneke started digging around in Elishia's sandbox with her hands. Sheera rushed over to help. Together they made a big pile of sand in the middle of the box.

"Why can't things ever stay the way they are?" she asked her dog. "No more changes! All I want...I just want to go camping with Ken. And that's all!"

She turned around to talk to Larry, but he was gone. Eileen told her she just missed him. He had left to get Elishia from Gram and Grump's. Annoyed, Anneke went up to her bedroom. Larry said he would talk, and then when she wanted him he was gone. She kicked the dresser leg. How could they even *think* she would just replace Mother. Never!

When Larry came back, dinner was ready. During a silent moment, Anneke said, "The Unos and Darryl are going camping. I'm invited."

"Who's Darryl?" Eileen asked.

"Mrs. Uno's new boyfriend. He camps a lot."

"Why would they want you to come along?" Larry asked.

"I found a valuable Japanese carving that might be part of her set. So Mrs. Uno invited me."

"Really? Where did you find this Japanese carving?" Eileen asked, standing up to pour more milk into Elishia's glass. "More?" she asked Anneke.

"Yes." Anneke held up her glass. "I found it in the river." Excitedly she started to talk about her adventure. But as soon as she got to the part where she had been swept up by the wild waves, she wished she hadn't said so much.

"The Slocan River?" Larry asked.

"Yes."

"Where it's wild enough to sweep you off your feet?" Larry looked grim.

Anneke could have kicked herself. She should have kept her big mouth shut! And why did Larry have to zoom in on her with the others around? Didn't he, of all people, know by now that Anneke was quite capable of looking after herself?

"What were you doing in the river?" Larry asked.

"Swimming." Anneke tried to sound nonchalant. "It was hot. Ken and Sheera and I went to the beach. Remember, I asked you? You said we could go. We saw this really neat red carving there, just washed up on a gravel bank. So I waded in and got it."

"Why did you get swept off your feet?" Larry wasn't fooled easily.

"I slipped."

Larry shook his head. "It sounds to me like the water you were in was pretty rough. It sounds like you weren't using your brain."

"I was! I wanted the carving. I knew exactly what I was doing."

But Larry, his voice getting louder, said, "Sometimes I wonder! You have to act more responsibly." His hand came down hard on the table.

"How can we trust you to go camping when you act so impulsively all the time?" Eileen put in.

"I don't *all* the time," Anneke snapped.

Eileen continued, looking at Larry, "We don't even know this man, Darryl."

Just then Elishia managed to dump her milk all

over the dinner table. Anneke could have hugged her, because while Eileen cleaned up the mess, Larry excused himself and went to the living room. Quickly Anneke followed.

"I'll talk to Mrs. Uno," he said. "Before I say *no!*" There was a big frown on his face.

"Ken says that Darryl is really nice," Anneke said. "And Ken really, really wants me to come."

"We'll see." Larry dialed the number and talked to Mrs. Uno, asking questions about her plans. Mostly he listened, Anneke noticed. Finally he said he'd get back to her and put the phone down. Running his hand through his thinning blond hair, he looked at Anneke for a while before saying, "Mrs. Uno loves the carving. She says it's a piece of Japanese art called a netsuke. She wants to check it out at the New Denver Nikkei Centre. She says you're the whole reason they're going there in the first place. She says you have the netsuke." He rubbed his head some more and looked up at the ceiling as if answers to his thoughts were written there.

Nervously Anneke tapped her fingers on the sides of her shorts. "I can help Darryl teach the Unos everything that you taught me," she said.

But Larry was unconvinced. "You don't seem to have learned much yourself. I certainly didn't teach you to risk your life in a wild river. I taught you to respect the fast-flowing parts. There are hidden logs under the surface. You *know* that! You could have gotten trapped underwater. You need to *think* before you act."

"I will! I'll stay with them all the time, and I'll do exactly as they say. You know Mrs. Uno. She won't even let Ken come over here by himself."

Larry relaxed a little. "That's true. You'll be under very watchful eyes. Maybe they'll teach *you* something instead. Maybe you'll come back all tamed." He actually smiled a little.

Anneke rolled her eyes. "Yeah, right."

"OK, you can go, if you promise to stay out of trouble. And show me that carving you found. Mrs. Uno sounded pretty excited about it."

"I will. I'll pack first," Anneke said quickly. "Can you phone Mrs. Uno back, and then tell Eileen?" She hurried up to her bedroom. She would show the Japanese god only to Larry, later, in her workshop.

On Friday Gram and Grump came by right on time to get Anneke for the corn barbecue with Mother. With her hands scrubbed, her hair freshly washed, and wearing clean shorts and T-shirt, Anneke followed Sheera into the car's back seat.

At the group home Mother sat outside on a bench in the shade, her beautiful hair gleaming almost as much as the gold-coloured clips she wore in it. Around her neck hung a matching necklace.

"Come and see my flowers," she said, taking Anneke's hand. They went around to the side of the building. "I planted these begonias yesterday. We bought them already blooming like this, so I kind of feel like I cheated. But don't they look beautiful?"

Anneke felt so happy, she hugged her mother.

Not because of the flowers. Of course the orange and yellow begonias were pretty, but Mother was even prettier, especially with that huge smile on her face. Mother was having a good day today.

"Let's show them to Gram and Grump," Anneke said. "Gram loves flowers."

Grump and Gram both made a big, happy fuss over the flowers. Grump even got his camera from the car to take a picture of Mother and Anneke pretending to weed the begonias.

"I can't find a single weed," Anneke said.

Mother bent towards her and kissed her cheek. Grump's camera clicked again.

"Let's invite Larry, Eileen, and Elishia over too," Grump said. "Today is a perfect day for a big, extended-family corn barbecue."

When Gram walked with Mother to the other side of the car, Grump whispered in Anneke's ear, "Now might be a good time to talk to your mom about the adoption idea."

Adoption? No! What business was it of Grump's to remind her of what she didn't want to think about? Then she remembered that Eileen told her it was Grump's idea in the first place. Did he want her as a *real* granddaughter? But then, he had Elishia already. And a new baby soon, while Mother would be all alone and...Mother was having a good day. Mother was better. Now was the perfect time to get Mother to rent a place and have Anneke and Sheera move back in with her.

In the front seat Gram and Grump were talking

about stopping to pick up Larry, Eileen, and Elishia. While the radio played music, Anneke snuggled closer to Mother on the back seat.

"When are you going to rent your own place again?" she whispered. "Sheera, get down," she added as the dog stuck her wet nose between the two faces. Like a sliding drop of water, a slither of excitement crept slowly down Anneke's spine: Mother looked wide awake; her eyes were clear.

She smiled at Anneke and, carefully, put her arm around her. "I need to talk to you about that, Kindeke. I won't be living on my own. I'm staying at the group home. I've been hired as a part-time worker there, in exchange for rent and food."

Anneke's excitement splattered to pieces as her hands gripped Sheera's fur. "But what about us?" she breathed.

"You know, Kindeke, I love you." Mother's eyes suddenly had tears in them. "I want so much to be with you. I think of you all the time, and I miss you when you're not around."

"We'll be together." Anneke's hopes soared. "You can work at the group home and live with me and Sheera. I'll get us a place."

At the mention of her name, the dog started to wriggle her way up between them again. Anneke kissed the soft doggie fur. "It'll be like before," she whispered.

"No, Kindeke. Dr. Sunnybrook says I have to stay where I am. She says things can't ever be like they were before. It's too risky for you, she says. You can't live with me. I have to listen to my doctor."

"But, Mama, you're better. Look. Your hands aren't even shaking a little!"

"I know. I feel much better. But you are happy at Larry and Eileen's, aren't you?"

"I am, mostly. Larry is great. Elishia's OK too, I guess. But Eileen's always busy with Elishia and her garden and Gram and Grump. She doesn't really have a lot of time for me. She leaves everything to Larry. And now she's pregnant. I want *you* to be my mother."

"I am. I will always be your mother. They want to adopt you. Everybody tells me that's best." Mother put her hands over her ears as if she didn't want to hear any more. "Everybody," she mumbled. "All the voices." Her hands started trembling slightly.

"Sheera, *get down!*" Anneke yelled, shoving the dog.

Her pet whimpered in surprise and slunk down on her belly to the floor of the car, staring up at Anneke.

Gram turned. She looked at Anneke, at Mother who was now shaking her head, at Sheera cowering. "Let's just have lunch with the four of us," she said to Grump. "We're almost there." She touched Anneke's arm.

Sheera was again slowly working her way up from the floor. She put her head in Anneke's lap and stared unblinkingly at her owner.

You're my best pal, Anneke thought, stroking the black-and-white head. At least you and I are always together. And Mother doesn't really want me to be adopted. I can tell. Next week Mother will be even better than today. Then we'll talk again.

CHAPTER 5

On Saturday morning, in the bright sunshine, the Unos, in Darryl's big Ford truck, came by to pick Anneke up. She noticed that, like her, Darryl wore old clothes, hiking shorts, and a T-shirt that said *Save Our Drinking Water*. He was clean-shaven, but his unruly brown hair was held down by a black baseball cap. Ken and his mom wore nice, clean clothes while Ken's big, fancy digital watch shone on his brown arm.

"Do you have the netsuke?" Mrs. Uno asked.

"Oh yes," Anneke said, patting her pocket.

She climbed into the back seat beside her friend, her long legs sticking up against the passenger's seat, a bandage still decorating her scraped knee. Sheera sat on the floor of the cab. All the gear was stored in the back, under a tarp.

They drove to New Denver in the hot sun and headed to the beach first, to have a swim and some lunch.

"That's Valhalla Park." Anneke pointed to the other side of the water. "Larry and I hiked up there once. To that waterfall. See over there, that white line? That's water. Was it ever a tough trail!"

"No kidding. It looks impossible," Ken groaned.

"We camped on the other side of the lake too," Anneke continued. "Before and after the hike. Right there, see...on that yellow patch of sandy beach. We were out in the open, with only a tarp over top of us, hung from tree to tree. And we had to hoist our food up over a tree branch, you know, to keep the bears from getting it."

Ken's eyes got bigger as Anneke bragged, but Mrs. Uno said, "I hope there aren't any bears at the campsite. I forgot about that."

Oops, Anneke thought. She looked at Darryl, who smiled at Ken's mom.

"We'll put all the food in the cab of the truck," he said. "We'll be fine."

After lunch they drove to the Nikkei Internment Memorial Centre and the adults bought tickets for everyone. "Follow this map and guide," the man said, handing them a brochure.

Mrs. Uno asked the ticket man if a member of the Kyowakai Society might possibly be available to look at the netsuke.

"Please stop in at the office afterwards," he said. "One of our seniors may have time to come over."

The Centre showed the shacks where Nikkei, Canadians of Japanese heritage, had lived during and after the Second World War. The brochure explained that thousands of Nikkei had been rounded up like cattle in Vancouver and other places along the coast of British Columbia. They were shipped by train to different places in the interior of B.C.

"Why?" Anneke looked at the tiny, three-room shack where ten to twelve people had been forced to live like prisoners.

"Because Canada was fighting against Japan in the Second World War," Mrs. Uno explained. "The Canadian government said all Nikkei needed to be evacuated. Of course we all *look* Japanese."

"But they were born in Canada, like my mom. Like me," Ken put in.

"That's discrimination," Anneke burst out. "Just because somebody looks different, or acts different..." She wasn't sure how to go on. But she noticed that they all nodded their heads in agreement.

Her eyes took in the thin walls with cracks, the hard wooden beds with old, grey army blankets. "And they made them all live *here*?" she asked quietly. "How would twelve people ever fit into this tiny space?"

"It was inhumane," Mrs. Uno said. "Families were broken up because the men and older boys were forced to build roads, or harvest sugar beets on Prairie farms. The women, children, and elderly were shipped out to camps like this one. Thousands ended up in West Kootenay ghost towns, where nothing was left except empty buildings, or they were even deposited in empty fields." She wiped her forehead with a fine lace handkerchief as the sun beamed down its summer heat.

"About 1500 Nikkei were dumped off here in 1942," she continued, "when New Denver was a tiny town of only a few hundred people. They came in a cold, cold winter. There was no electricity. And no stoves. Not even running water. They weren't used to the cold, and they only got two blankets each." Mrs. Uno hugged her arms around herself and shivered as if an icy hand had just brushed across her bare arms. She swallowed hard and continued, "At first they lived in tents. Then they built these shacks."

Ken said, "Both my grandparents' families *had to* move here. Ojisan, that's my grandfather, and Obasan weren't married yet. They all had big houses in Vancouver. And cars. And Ojisan's dad had a cool fishing boat. They had lots of nice things. The government grabbed all their stuff, *everything*." Ken's voice got louder and he waved his arms as he went on. "They just took it all and sold it. They used the money to pay for the camps. Nobody even got their own stuff back!"

Mrs. Uno said, "That's why I'm so excited about the netsuke. It may be a part of our family treasure from the days before the Second World War."

Anneke's hand flew down and into her pocket. Hotei was securely resting at the bottom of it. She buttoned the pocket again.

The group stood silently while everyone looked at the skinny double-bunk beds, the water buckets, the small outhouse used by as many as fifty people.

Finally Darryl put his arm around Mrs. Uno's shoulder and asked, "Were your parents OK?"

Mrs. Uno said, "My dad and grandfather were forced to build roads. My grandfather got tuberculosis, so he was sent here, to the sanitarium. But he never got better. He died the next year." Mrs. Uno wiped her face again, especially her eyes, Anneke noticed. Then she continued, "Finally, towards the end of the Second World War, my dad was allowed to join his family."

Anneke felt herself breathe a sigh of relief. At least they were together, finally, after a long, difficult time. She touched the netsuke in her pocket. She'd give it to Ken's mom if it turned out to be one of the pieces of her set.

Mrs. Uno went on, "After the war my family was told to move to Alberta."

Darryl interrupted. "You mean even *after* the war they weren't allowed to do what they wanted?"

"No, not for about four years. But finally, when they were no longer treated like prisoners, my parents moved to Rock Creek. They were only allowed to go up to grade eight in the school at the camp, so they worked really hard and sent me to university."

Anneke moved over to Ken. "Do your grandparents still live in Rock Creek?" she whispered, sensing somehow that speaking too loudly would break the bond they all felt.

"No, Ojisan died before I was born," Ken said. "Obasan died two years ago."

"Thank you for bringing me here," Darryl said,

taking Mrs. Uno's hand. The adults looked sombre as they walked on to another shack. Anneke and Ken moved over to the Peace Arch that took up the far corner. They didn't talk; they just stood side by side, looking up at the arch.

The ticket man walked over to the adults. "Mr. Kubota has arrived," he announced. "He is anxious to see the carving."

They all hurried to the front office and eagerly crowded around a man with very short grey hair who stood leaning on a cane. After introductions, Mr. Kubota took the small object from Anneke and held it up to a light.

"What can you tell me about this?" he inquired.

Mrs. Uno told him how Anneke had found the object in the river, and how she herself had four of the seven carvings of the gods of luck at home. "My netsuke came from Japan many years ago," she said. "I have Benten, Ebisu, Jurojin, and Bishamon. I know my parents valued them highly. They said for them this treasure represented family and happiness." She carefully pushed her black hair back from her face.

Mr. Kubota nodded. He stroked the shiny wood with a finger, mumbling something Anneke didn't understand.

Mrs. Uno continued, "My father told me once that there is another family, distant relatives of my mother who has the other three gods from my set. The two families were neighbours in Vancouver. They wanted to stay together here, in one of these shacks. But the relatives were forced to move on to

Greenwood. Before our families were separated, they divided the seven gods of luck among themselves and hid them. They vowed that someday they would meet again. They never did. But I wonder, could this carving, Hotei, be one of those netsuke? Why was Hotei in the river? And where is the other family now? My parents never talked about their time here very much."

Mr. Kubota looked up. "I understand," he said. "Many families didn't want to talk about their horrendous experiences."

"My parents are dead now," Mrs. Uno added. "I tried to find this other family, even before my mother died. I thought back then that it would pull her out of her depression: she lost so much. But even now that she is gone—*especially* now that she is gone— I would like to find the owners of this netsuke."

Mr. Kubota nodded again. He studied the object carefully through a magnifying glass, then opened an old book to the back pages. Anneke saw Japanese characters instead of words made with letters from the alphabet. She moved even closer, peering over Ken's shoulder.

"Information," Mr. Kubota said, holding the book for them to see. "All about our many years here in New Denver. Some of the older Society members and I wrote down a lot of details about what we remembered of our lives in the 1940s, 50s, and 60s."

He flipped through some pages, his eyes scanning the characters quickly, his finger moving up and down the rows. Finally he shook his head and said, "I don't know. Nothing is mentioned about a carved wooden set of seven gods. But of course many Nikkei didn't tell their story to us. With your permission I will make a few inquiries in the Society." He gave the object back to Anneke. "Please stay in touch," he nodded.

After Mr. Kubota and Mrs. Uno exchanged phone numbers, Mrs. Uno suggested that Anneke put the netsuke in the truck's glove compartment. Then she changed her mind, deciding that if for some reason they were robbed at the campsite at night, thieves would look there first.

Darryl laughed and said, "The only robbers at campsites are squirrels, raccoons, and other animals. I can see we have a lot to teach these two." He winked at Anneke, who quietly slid the netsuke back into her deep hiking shorts pocket and buttoned it up.

"That is a really cool place," she said to Ken. "You get to see what happened to your family."

"It's real Canadian history," he replied importantly. "I've read a lot about it."

"I guess you would have," Anneke grinned. "I wish I could..." she stopped. She knew nothing about her own family, only about Mother, who had, as a young woman, come to Canada from Holland. She had come alone, with, she insisted, no relatives left alive in Holland. And Mother had always forbidden Anneke to ask about her father or her father's parents. Some day, Anneke decided, she'd find out more about her own relatives.

CHAPTER 6

The drive to Rosebery was short. Everybody helped to set up camp. Ken and his mom each had their own small, brand-new, dome tents. Darryl had a small, ultra-lightweight tent, while Anneke and Sheera would sleep in Larry's family tent.

By the time Anneke had set up her tent by herself and laid out her foamy, sleeping bag, pillow, and Sheera's blanket, Darryl already had his tent up, as well as Mrs. Uno's. While he helped Ken snap his poles together, Mrs. Uno took her overnight bag from the truck.

"I'll just sort things out over here and get them ready for the tent," she said to Anneke, putting a makeup bag, hand lotion, and a box of biscuits on the picnic table.

"Larry never allows anything that smells in a tent," Anneke said. "Because of bears."

"Everything is in containers," Mrs. Uno said.

But Darryl, after showing Ken how to hammer

the pegs in by himself, told Mrs. Uno that Anneke was right. "No biscuits," he said. "Really, if you want to be sure, no toothpaste or lotion either. Bears have an amazing sense of smell."

"Toothpaste?" Mrs. Uno's eyes got bigger.

"Of course if the bear eats the toothpaste first, his breath won't be so bad," Darryl quipped.

"I don't know..." Mrs. Uno looked around her at the tall trees and the shrubs. "Maybe..." She started putting her belongings back into her overnight bag.

"You'll be safe if you play it safe," Darryl assured her. "Give bears no reason for a midnight visit and they'll leave you alone. Put your bag in the truck's cab and take it into the tent tomorrow morning after you get up."

Mrs. Uno didn't look at all reassured. "But if a bear..." She stopped, then added, "Will you lock the cab?"

"I could," Darryl said. "But bears usually don't have drivers' licences."

"Oh you." Mrs. Uno gave his shoulder a little push as she smiled.

"Don't worry," Darryl said. "We'll be fine."

"I hope I can sleep tonight." Ken held up a bent tent peg. "Look at this."

Darryl laughed. "Yes, those metal toothpicks they call tent pegs are no good. Here, I always use old railway spikes or extra-large nails. I have lots." He helped Ken secure his tent to the ground.

Mrs. Uno put her bag in the cab and started fussing with the picnic table. First she brought out a tablecloth and clips. Then she produced a vase.

"Where are the taps?" she asked.

"There's a pump. We came past it at the entrance," Darryl said.

"But the bathrooms must have water taps," Mrs. Uno said.

"No bathrooms," Anneke said. "There are outhouses."

Mrs. Uno looked ready to pack up and go home. Darryl said, "Here, you kids get us some water." He handed two buckets to Ken and Anneke.

Ken liked cranking the pump handle. He and Anneke had a contest to see who could pump the fattest stream of water. At first Anneke won, but in the end Ken had caught on and could pump harder and faster. By the time the buckets were full, the two friends were both soaked and laughing so hard they could hardly carry the water up the hill to their site.

"Let's go to the lake," Anneke said.

"Mom won't let us I bet."

Ken was right. Mrs. Uno decided that they could go for a short walk, but not to the lake.

"Don't go too far," she stressed.

"You'll have to be back soon anyway," Darryl said. "I expect you two to chop wood and start a fire in a while. And you'd better bring good appetites. I'm making a big pot of woodsman's soup with dumplings *and* a quick jambalaya."

Anneke looked up. "A quick what?" she asked.

"A jum-ba-la-ya. It's a rice dish with meat and vegetables."

Anneke said nothing, but wrinkled up her nose.

She didn't like rice nearly as much as macaroni and cheese.

Ken looked happy. "My mom brought peach pie and whipped cream for dessert," he said. "We're going to eat well tonight. Let's go."

They started down a trail that passed behind their site with Sheera, as always, in the lead, her tail wagging hard.

"Watch out for bears," Mrs. Uno called as they rounded a curve.

"Ah," Anneke said, slapping Ken on the shoulder. "A hike, a fire, peach pie, and a night in a tent: this is the way I like to spend my weekend."

"I guess." He didn't seem quite as sure about it all as she was.

Early the next morning Anneke woke to Sheera's wet nose sniffing her cheek.

"Hi, pooch," she whispered. "Go on then, outside with you." She knew that her pet wouldn't leave her alone now until she opened the tent's zipper.

Mrs. Uno was already at the picnic table, her overnight bag beside her, a mirror propped up against an empty cooking pot. She was rubbing something on her face. Curious, Anneke crawled out of her tent and walked over. "Ouch," she said as she stepped on a pine cone with her bare foot.

"Good morning. I just finished my face." Mrs. Uno put her comb and all her little containers back into her bag. "How did you sleep?"

"Fine." Anneke always slept well when she went camping. "How about you?"

Mrs. Uno shrugged her shoulders. "Sleeping on the ground takes a bit of getting used to. Somebody snored most of the night."

"Oh, that was probably Sheera. She's a terrible snorer. When we all go camping, Eileen always calls in the middle of the night for Sheera to turn over. So I poke her and then she stops snoring for a while."

Mrs. Uno smiled, but asked, "How can you sleep through the noise?"

"I'm used to it." Looking around for her dog, Anneke saw Sheera sniffing furiously at something. When she walked over, she saw a pile of fresh deer droppings.

"We had a visitor during the night," she called to Mrs. Uno.

"A bear?" Mrs. Uno grabbed her bag, quickly put it in the truck's cab, and closed the door. "There," she said.

Anneke chuckled. "It was a deer." She returned to her tent, saying, "I'll get dressed."

After putting on her bathing suit, shorts, T-shirt, and shoes, she rolled up and tied her sleeping bag, foamy, and Sheera's blanket together. She put them with her pillow at the tent's entrance, ready to be loaded onto the truck. Darryl was chopping kindling. Ken's tent bulged out on one side, then on the other.

"Are you exercising in there?" Anneke joked as she walked past.

"This stupid tent's too small," Ken grumbled. "I'm trying to get dressed. I keep falling over when I try to get my shorts on."

"Lie down then," Anneke said. She couldn't wait to tell Larry about this trip. They'd have a good chuckle together. Especially when she told him how Mrs. Uno had brought a little mat to put under her lawn chair. To keep the mud off her shoes, she had explained, although it hadn't rained for days and things were super dry in the Kootenays. But last night, every time the campfire's smoke blew in her direction, Mrs. Uno had picked up her chair *and* the mat to move to the other side of the firepit. The wind had been especially mischievous, and Mrs. Uno had played her version of musical chairs until Darryl suggested the two of them go for a walk and leave the kids to tend the fire. They'd only been gone for a few minutes when they came back because Mrs. Uno needed to change her shoes. Then they returned to get a flashlight. And again, a bit later, Mrs. Uno needed a long-sleeved shirt. Ken and Anneke had stayed by the fire all evening, toasting marshmallows, telling each other stories and jokes, howling to the moon, and keeping the fire going.

Now Anneke asked Darryl if he wanted her to make a breakfast fire. "I'm good at it," she boasted. "Larry taught me."

Darryl handed her the kindling and matches. "Larry must be great to camp with."

"He is." Anneke crumpled two newspapers, built a little teepee of sticks over them, and struck a match. "Do you need flames or hot coals to cook on?" she asked.

"Neither. Ken's mom wanted a little fire for atmosphere." Darryl set a bag of granola on the table.

"Larry never lets us make a fire in the morning if we don't need it to cook on."

"I know," Darryl shrugged. "I don't usually either. Never mind."

They all sat around the picnic table to eat breakfast while the fire burned itself out.

"Let's rent canoes," Darryl said.

It looked as though it would be another hot day, so everyone agreed that being out on the water was a good idea. They packed up the site and left the loaded truck along the road near the entrance to the campground. The beach was close by and soon two canoes glided over the water, Darryl and Mrs. Uno's lagging behind farther and farther while Anneke and Ken pushed their craft forward with big, strong strokes.

"Sheera, sit," Anneke said again. "Stay."

The dog wanted to go for a swim. She whined when, close by, a fish jumped out of the water, arched, and splashed back down.

"Let's head for that beach." Anneke pointed her paddle. Ken nodded.

Soon the bow scraped on the sand. When they looked back, the lake was empty. Darryl and Mrs. Uno had not yet rounded the bluff that stuck out into the lake.

CHAPTER 7

Anneke and Sheera went for a quick swim. Ken, getting wet up to his knees, decided that the water was freezing cold. Finally the adults rounded the bluff, and soon Darryl joined Anneke for another swim.

They ate lunch, played on the beach, and in the afternoon paddled back to Rosebery.

"Before we head home, do you want to join us for a snack at the Wild Rose?" Mrs. Uno asked.

"Let's go exploring," Anneke said.

Ken looked unsure. "What are you having at the restaurant?" he asked his mother.

"Hey, you two could finish up that last half of the peach pie and whipped cream," Darryl said. "It's in the cooler, in the back of the truck. Exploring sounds like fun."

"I don't know, Darryl," Mrs. Uno said. "We just went exploring all day."

"But they'll have to sit long enough on the way

back," Darryl said. "We're just having a drink. Don't worry," he added quickly to Mrs. Uno: "you can drink pop and drive."

"Me, drive that big truck of yours?"

"Sure." Darryl tickled Mrs. Uno's neck. "If you go out with a big bad bozo like me, you'll have to toughen up a little sooner or later." He slipped his arm around her shoulder.

Mrs. Uno giggled. "Well...," she said, allowing Darryl to turn her in the direction of the Wild Rose.

"Have fun," Darryl said, looking over his shoulder.

"We will," Anneke said. "Ken has a watch. We'll be at the truck at...what time?"

"At five," Darryl said.

Mrs. Uno checked her watch. "That's almost an hour, Darryl. That's far too much time."

"They'll be fine. They know where we are."

Anneke and Ken ate the pie with loads of whipped cream and washed it down with water from the pump. Then they set off along the trail by the river.

Anneke stopped at the next bend and called Sheera back. "Phew," she groaned. "I ate too much."

Ken sat down on a rock, breathing heavily. "Me too. Darryl sure wanted to get rid of us."

"I guess." Anneke grinned and looked at the fast-flowing water. "I wonder what's on the other side."

Ken sighed. "Did you see how he just gets Mom to do whatever he wants?"

"Yeah, but your mom's always so careful. Let's

go across the river."

"Are you crazy?" Ken stared at her. "It's wilder here than where you almost drowned the other day."

"So? Almost drowned isn't the same as drowned. You sound like Larry. He doesn't think I can look after myself either. Don't tell me *you* want to be my dad too."

"Me?" Ken burst out. "No way!" He slapped at a mosquito on his arm, then scratched. "I'd be your mom's husband." He snickered, but stopped quickly when all he got was a dirty look.

"Mother wants to stay..." Anneke left the unfinished sentence suspended in the air like a broken tree branch.

"I hope Darryl doesn't start hanging around *all* the time," Ken said. "I *have* a dad. He lives in California. I see him once a year. I don't need two dads."

"That's exactly how I feel." Anneke slapped a mosquito extra hard. "I have a mother. I don't need two."

"But," Ken said, "your mom can't live with you. My mom says you're better off the way you are now, with Larry and Eileen."

"They want to adopt me." The words slipped out before Anneke could stop herself. She wasn't sure she wanted Ken to know.

"I hope Darryl doesn't want to marry Mom and adopt *me*." Ken picked a bit of dried moss off his shirt.

"He's an OK guy," Anneke said. "And your dad lives far away. Not like Eileen and my mother. They both live here."

"But..." Ken frowned. Then he added with great certainty, "If they want to adopt you, I'd let them."

"So why is adoption OK for me but not for you?" Anneke felt anger rising. "Is it because my mother has schizophrenia? Because if that's what you're thinking..." She jumped up and started walking away.

"No, no," Ken said, catching up. "All I meant was that Larry and Eileen are sort of cool. And you really like Larry."

"So? I like Darryl, too," Anneke snapped. "At least he doesn't try to preach to you about 'using your brain' in front of your mother." She kicked a pebble that went flying into the water.

Walking fast, she came to a bend in the river where a big fallen tree spanned the water like a bridge.

"Let's go across."

But Ken wasn't so sure. "Why?" he asked, a frown on his face.

"To look around on the other side of course."

"It'll be the same as here." Ken scratched his leg.

But Anneke pointed across the river and up the hill. "Way up there is a park that's really wild. They say there's a cabin there somewhere. They say it's haunted."

She started balancing herself on the tree, arms out, when she remembered she'd promised Larry to be careful around rivers. Just a quick look, she thought. Besides, why should Larry tell her what she could and could not do? Everyone wanted to organize her life. Even Mother was in on the plan now. *Mother!* And she was supposed to be on Anneke's side. Taking several slow, sliding steps on the wet, slippery wood, she called, "It's easy."

"It sure doesn't look easy," Ken said.

She glanced over her shoulder and saw him sitting on a big rock, Sheera beside him. He shook his head when she called, "Come on."

With both her arms stretched out for balance, she slid along, concentrating on her feet, getting closer to the middle of the rushing river.

More than halfway across, the tree narrowed. Anneke took another small step forward. Another. By this time the log was only a bit wider than her shoe. She wouldn't be able to turn around now even if she wanted to. Another step. The tree narrowed more. Just a bit farther and she'd be on the other side. Her shoe slid forward. She wobbled. Stopping to find her balance, she held her arms out like wings, her body teetering from side to side.

After regaining her balance, she moved forward again. Then, with a big leap, Anneke jumped onto the bank, barely reaching the sand. Scrambling quickly to higher ground, she felt a few pebbles loosening and rolling into the river right behind her heels.

Triumphantly she turned. "Nothing to it." She waved Ken over.

Sheera barked and ran back and forth along the bank. Ken sat, shaking his head. He said something.

"What?" Anneke yelled back. The river rushed loudly.

He called again, but she still couldn't hear what he said. Shrugging, she cupped her hands around her mouth and called as loudly as she could, "Sheera. Come."

The dog barked, took two steps on the tree, retreated and then ran back and forth along the bank again, barking.

"I'll just explore a bit," Anneke yelled, pointing to the woods behind her, knowing Ken couldn't hear what she said. She scrambled all the way up the bank and walked into the trees. The woods on this side looked much the same as on the other side, although there was no path along the river. Clambering onto an old, fallen, half-rotten trunk, she scanned the area. Dense forest spread around her: tall trees, some old and with long, dry strings of old-man's-beard lichen hanging from the branches, low shrubs, a few prickly brambles, fallen branches, pine cones, and a thick carpet of needles. Here and there the sun's rays created light patches of brilliant green in the otherwise darker shade.

Anneke walked a bit farther along, avoiding the huge leaves and spiky stems of some giant devil's club. She climbed up onto a big rock outcropping that lay exposed to the sun; then she stood and, shading her eyes with one hand, studied her surroundings slowly. Woods, woods, and more woods.

Surprised that Sheera hadn't found a way to cross the river by now, Anneke sat down to wait for a while. Her pet was always by her side and she felt a bit unsettled without the dog. I'll go back, she thought, swatting at a big, annoying black fly. It wouldn't be easy though. The skinny part of the tree was on this side of the river. But she'd manage somehow.

Just as she jumped up, she heard a happy woof. Sheera, soaking wet, had found her.

A noise from farther behind startled both of them, a noise of nails scurrying on bark. Sheera growled, ran around a thick clump of growth, and over to a pine tree. Anneke followed. When she looked up she saw a black ball of fur, the body of an animal smaller than her dog. A little face with a cute pointy snout stuck out from the fur. Two frightened eyes looked down at them.

"Sheera, no," Anneke said.

The dog barked, her front paws up on the tree trunk, her eyes never leaving the body of the wild creature high up on the branch.

"Sheera, no! It's a bear cub." Anneke petted the dog to calm her down. "A lonely little cub. Oh look, Sheera, she's so cute. She must only have been born this last winter."

And then the cub cried, a sound so lonely, so lost and frightened that Anneke reached her arms up as if to encourage the cub to jump down into an embrace. "Oh," she whispered. "You want your mama."

The mama bear! She'd come crashing through

the trees any moment now, ready to attack and maul both Anneke and Sheera.

"Come," she whispered urgently. "We have to get out of here."

But Sheera didn't want to follow. Anneke had to take the dog by the collar and pull her away from the tree. The little cub cried again, the call sounding almost like a human baby's. Dragging her pet away, Anneke scanned the area. No mother bear yet. If she hurried, she might be safe. Pulling the unwilling dog along, she came to a big fallen log. Sheera wouldn't jump over it. Anneke, frustrated, yelled, "Move it, Sheera. Now!" The dog heard the anxiety in her owner's voice. She barked louder. Jerking free from Anneke's grasp, she sped back to the tree where the cub was perched.

Any second now the angry sow would come crashing through the shrubs, ready to kill whoever threatened her little one. Anneke squeezed her eyes shut in fear. What could she do? How could she protect her own "little one" against an angry sow? She couldn't.

"Sheera, come," she almost cried. "No! Come." Of all the times for her pet to disobey! Anneke knew she should leave, but she couldn't, wouldn't, abandon her dog.

And then, for the third time, the cub cried, a sound so lonely, so helpless, so frightened, it seared through Anneke like the pain of ripping something off her skin, like the pain of tearing something out of her body—like the pain of losing a mother. She wrapped her arms around herself and shivered. One big sob escaped from her chest.

Sheera was now whimpering, reaching as far up the tree as her front paws would go. Was the cub alone? Was the poor little thing up there starving? Why wasn't Sheera sniffing out the mother bear? If the sow *was* around, she would have rushed in by now. Bears had very keen noses and sharp ears.

Uncertain, Anneke stood, taking Sheera by the collar again. If the sow showed up, they wouldn't be able to outrun her. They'd have to play dead. If the bear didn't show up, the cub was alone and starving.

Anneke stood a little longer. Longer still, every muscle tense as a spring, ready for flight. Nothing moved.

After what seemed like forever, she knew the mother bear wouldn't show. She, Anneke, would have to rescue the little black ball. She couldn't leave a tiny orphan to fend for herself.

Standing motionless for another long moment, she considered her options. Sheera had to be kept away. Anneke herself couldn't coax the cub out of the tree. The little one was frightened, so she wouldn't come down for a long time, probably not for hours, maybe not all day.

Anneke decided her best option would be to mark the area, cross the river again, and get Darryl to phone someone. A vet maybe, or the police. No, the fire department. Firemen sometimes brought people's cats down from tall trees or telephone poles. No, better yet, Darryl would phone Larry. He would have gotten home from work by now. And Larry always knew how to handle these sorts of emergencies; he knew more about the outdoors than anyone else Anneke knew.

Larry would be furious when he found out that she had crossed a tree over a raging river, and that she could have been mauled by an angry bear. So be it. Anneke could only worry about one thing at a time, and right now there was a motherless cub to think about.

Looking up, she made some clucking sounds. "Don't worry," she said. "We'll get you down. You're lucky I found you. Hey, that's a good name for you. Lucky."

Searching her pockets for something to tie around the tree, she found only some shiny round pebbles from the New Denver beach, a few tissues, and Hotei, the little carved god. She decided to memorize the tree and its surrounding landmarks instead. Then she set off for the river, still holding onto Sheera's collar.

The dog kept looking back at the tree, whining from time to time. But Anneke resolutely dragged her pet away. "You can't always have what you want," she told the resisting animal. "Sheera! Quit it."

When she reached the big rock outcropping that she'd sat on earlier, she let go of the dog's collar and looked for signs of water glistening between the trees. Not yet, although the river should be right there, behind that thick growth of devil's club. Scrambling around the spiky stems and huge leaves, she heard water rushing. Aha, the river, she thought. But then she saw a small creek spilling down the hillside. The stream led to a little pool where the water circled round and round and round in a crazy eddy before plunging down a cliff farther along, creating a stringy waterfall. The little pool made a convenient drinking place for animals; Anneke noticed tracks leading away from the pool and up the hillside. She spotted some fresh and some old animal droppings. There was no sign that a bear had been around here though.

Where *was* the mother bear? Could she have been injured? Or shot by hunters? By poachers? Anneke knew some people killed wild animals illegally. But she hadn't noticed signs of bears in this whole area, other than the cub. No overturned rocks, no parts of rotting trees pulled apart, no paw prints in the soil or fresh claw marks on trees.

While she watched Sheera having a drink, her stomach tightened. This stream and this pool were not here on her way up the hill. She hadn't seen any animal tracks on her way up either. Walking back around the devil's club she listened for the roar of the river. All she heard was the little creek and the whirl of water in the pool.

Where was the river? Where was the tree with the cub even? These tall trees all looked the same. The rock outcropping she had sat on was nowhere to be seen. She walked a little in one direction, then another. Woods, woods, woods.

"Sheera, come." Anneke started running and scrambling down the hill but was stopped by a short, very steep cliff. She turned and ran back up the hill, Sheera following, scampering happily as if it were a game of hide-and-seek.

"Sheera, where's the bear? Go find." She might as well start from that tree again, Anneke decided.

The dog, nose to the ground, tail wagging, started up the hill. Soon she barked and stretched her front paws up a tree. The cub had moved farther up into the branches, but Anneke was glad to see the tree again.

She stood with her back turned to the trunk and scanned the area. She'd come from over there. No. Over that way. Actually, no, more to the right. Although those shrubs that looked like wild huckleberries weren't there before. So that wasn't the way back. But neither was the area to the left.

Slowly the realization sank in. She had no idea where the river was: she was lost.

CHAPTER 8

Leaning more heavily against the tree trunk, Anneke clearly heard Larry's words in her head. *If you ever get lost in the woods, stay put. Don't get more lost. Stay in one place and let people find you.*

"Well, baby bear," she called up, "you won't be alone. We'll let the adults find all of us together. Darryl should be here in an hour or so."

Sitting down on a mossy patch under a nearby tree, she called Sheera over. The dog rested her head on Anneke's lap, looking at her mistress, then at the cub. Suddenly, from above their heads somewhere, a squirrel chicka-chicka-chicked her displeasure at the intrusion. Sheera scrambled to her feet and raced to a dead tree trunk that had fallen over and was leaning against a live tree as if it were part of a gym's climbing equipment. Without a second thought the dog ran up the slanted tree, trying to reach the squirrel. At the junction with the live tree, Sheera wobbled, tried to back up, then fell with a crash into a shrub below. She gave a surprised yip before she ran back to Anneke. Like a toddler, she held out her paw to be stroked and kissed better before she bounded off to another tree where the squirrel now sat on a higher branch, laughing.

A grey jay also spotted them. The bird sat on a low branch, its head moving back and forth, one curious eye staring at the two on the ground.

The moss on the forest floor smelled as fresh as spring shoots, even in the dryness of midsummer. Anneke lay down, put her nose right into the clump of tiny green plants, and breathed deeply.

"I wonder what time it is," she said to the animal world. "I might as well keep busy and carve something."

She got up and looked around for a solid chunk of wood. When she found one, she turned it slowly in her hands. Looking at it from one angle, the vague shape of a four-legged animal showed. From another angle Anneke saw the smooth back of a bear. A sow standing on her hind feet. A mother bear hugging her cub to her chest, the front legs wrapped around the little one. Taking the Swiss Army knife from her belt, Anneke started whittling the hind legs.

The knife kept slipping. Once Anneke almost cut her thumb. She wished she was at her workbench with the vise. She wished she had a picture of a bear. Then a sudden thought struck her. This carving didn't have to look exactly like a mother bear holding a cub. It could look like the *idea* of a big animal hugging a baby. The hugging part would be more important than the actual shape. The hugging, sort of like the way Eileen hugged, her arms wrapped around the other person, like little circles of safety. The *idea* of safety was what she wanted to carve. Like the netsuke Ken's mom had, the goddess that stood for art and love. Anneke stopped working on the bear's legs, turned the wood over, and started on the front.

A baby's face would peek out from the top of hugging arms. Any kind of face, as long as it was the same but smaller than the face of the adult. "This will be my goddess of safety," she told Sheera.

"Anneke?"

Sheera jumped up and ran towards a big fallen tree. Again Anneke heard her name. They had come for her already. That was quick. Then she saw Ken scrambling over the log, Sheera running circles around him.

"It's you. You crossed. *And* you found me!"

Ken leaned against a tree. "I waited and waited for you," he grumbled. "*What* are you doing here? We were supposed to meet Mom and Darryl at the truck by now."

"You mean you're not with Darryl?" Anneke asked.

"No. I crossed by myself. To tell you to get back there."

Anneke pointed up the tree. "Look what I found!"

Ken looked up too. "What is that? A black cat?"

"No, it's a cub. I'm going to rescue her."

"A bear. Oh man!" Ken looked a bit bewildered.

"She's tiny," Anneke said defensively. Just then the little snout pointed down at them.

"Oh, she *is* cute," Ken said.

"No kidding, eh," Anneke said. "I'm calling her Lucky."

"Why? What's so lucky about sitting up there and having people stare at you?" Then, suddenly, Ken's eyes showed fear. "Where's the mother bear?" He looked around frantically.

"Gone. But I'm going to rescue the cub. That's why she's lucky I came along."

"We sure won't be lucky when we get to the truck," Ken stated.

"What time is it?"

"Ten after five. We need to hurry. Mom will be having a fit."

"I got lost," Anneke said sheepishly, clipping her knife to her belt. "You lead the way."

"Me? I thought you—The river is down there somewhere." He pointed.

"Are you sure? Sheera saw you over there." Anneke pointed more to the right.

"No, I'm not sure. I kind of wandered back and forth for a while, trying to find you. Man, am I ever going to get it." Ken glanced at his watch again. "I should never have followed you. And it looked like the water in the river came up higher too. By the time I got across, the end part was a bit underwater."

"Oh, I forgot about that. It's afternoon on a hot summer's day," Anneke stated.

"So?" Ken said.

"So, the hot sun melts the glacial ice all day long and that water runs down the hills and swells the rivers a bit. Not as much as on rainy days though. Later on tonight the water will go down again."

"Later on tonight!" Ken almost yelled. "Are you waiting until then? Oh man!" He hit his fists on his shorts.

"Calm down," Anneke said. "Darryl will look for us."

"But not on *this* side of the river," Ken screamed. "They'll look on the other side. *Nobody* but you and harebrained me would cross on that tree. Why did I follow you?" He shook his head wildly.

Anneke realized that Ken was getting himself worked into a panic. He didn't have the experience she had in the outdoors. She had learned a lot from going out with Larry and from always having to think and stay calm with Mother. Ken usually played games at his computer or read books. *And* his mom was far stricter than Larry.

"We're not really all that lost," she tried, knowing she could be lying. "Let's just go and find the river. Then, if we can't cross back we can at least wave at them."

"Let's hurry," Ken said.

Anneke left her carving at the foot of the cub's tree, called up, "I'll be back soon," and followed Ken. They clambered over a log, moved around some devil's club, through some low shrubs, and over two more fallen logs. None of the trees looked familiar to Anneke. But then, these woods all looked the same. What worried her more was that she couldn't hear the sounds of the river rushing.

Sheera, who was ahead as always, started down

an animal track. Part of Anneke's brain screamed at her, "Stop! You're getting us more lost." But the part that wanted to keep her friend calm, together with that other part of her, that restless, adventurous part, won out. She moved on behind Sheera, almost at a run, down the animal track. Ken stuck close to them, she noticed.

Suddenly the narrow track started to climb steeply. Too late, Anneke realized she'd listened to the wrong voice in her brain. She stopped, called Sheera back, and said, "Ken, we can't keep going. We're lost and we'll get more lost. I'm sorry. I think I got you into *big* trouble."

"But the river should be—" Ken started.

"No," Anneke stopped him. "The river is big and wild enough that we can hear the rushing water a little ways up the hill. I don't hear anything, do you?"

"Maybe that way," Ken pointed. "I think I hear something."

They walked on a while, listening, searching through the trees for a glint of water. Nothing. Only woods and more woods.

Anneke stopped again and said, "Let's not go farther from the crossing tree. Let's get Sheera to lead us back to the bear cub. We'll wait there."

"How can the river just disappear?" Ken asked, his voice a bit shaky. "It was right there, at the bottom of that little hill."

"It's really easy to get lost," Anneke said. "Even Larry got lost once. We'll be fine if we do the smart thing. We'll stay at the tree with the cub."

"Aren't you scared?" Ken asked.

"Sort of. But I know we'll be found."

"How?"

"Larry. He'll find us."

Ken nodded, looking a bit relieved. "My mom will phone Larry. Maybe she already did. She says he's the best thing that ever happened to you. She thinks he's cool."

"He is." Anneke stroked Sheera's head, then told her pet to find the bear cub. She started the dog off down the animal track again, back in the direction they had come from.

Sheera, her nose to the ground, wagged her tail excitedly. She bounded this way and that. Suddenly she sped off the trail and through some shrubs.

Anneke looked just in time to see a deer leaping away through the trees.

"Ken, look," she pointed. But he had already spotted the mule deer.

"Sheera, no," Anneke called. She knew the dog would obey her only grudgingly. Stopping a chase on a running wild animal had been one of the hardest, but most important lessons for the border collie to learn. Now Sheera whimpered as she stopped chasing and watched the deer crash off through the woods. Soon it was gone.

Still excited, Sheera ran around the area, her nose to the ground.

"Good girl, Sheera. Find the bear. Where is it?" Anneke encouraged her. But, when she saw her pet only wanted to follow the mule deer, she added to her friend, "Sorry, Ken. Sheera won't look for the bear cub now. She's distracted by the deer smells."

Ken, suddenly sitting down hard on the ground as if his knees had simply given out, said, "What do we do?"

"We can stay here and wait for Larry and Darryl. But they may take quite a while. Darn." She hit her fists together.

"What?" Ken sounded anxious.

"My whistle," Anneke said. "It's in my survival kit. I always take it. But I thought we were just going camping."

"*So did I*!" Ken jumped up. "We can't just sit here and do nothing. I'm going to find the river."

"But wandering around'll just get you more lost," Anneke said.

"I'm not wandering. The river's down there somewhere," Ken pointed, setting out. "It can't be that far." He clambered over a fallen tree and crashed through some low shrubs.

"We have to stay together." Reluctantly Anneke called Sheera and followed.

Soon Ken stopped. A steep, short cliff gaped before him. Lower down, the woods continued. The river was nowhere to be seen; no sound of water rushing could be heard.

"There's a gravel road higher up." Anneke was thinking out loud, trying to remember all the places she and Larry had hiked or driven to. "It's on this side of the river. It goes up to a fishing lake, I think."

"Let's find it." Ken seemed eager.

"It'll take us farther away from the river," Anneke warned.

"But we'll be on a road," Ken said. "There'll be traffic."

"Not much," Anneke said. "Maybe none."

"It's getting late." Ken checked his watch again, something he'd been doing every few minutes. "It'll start to get dark soon."

"What time is it?"

"6:11"

"Oh, it won't be dark for several hours." Anneke glanced at Ken. She knew it was crazy to walk around in these endless woods, but Ken looked less worried when he kept moving. They started off again.

Soon Sheera found them a track that zigzagged uphill. Anneke pointed out the difference between the larger elk droppings and smaller deer droppings. Then she found even smaller rabbit droppings. Importantly she poked them with a little stick and passed on the information she'd learned from Larry. "The rabbit droppings are drier, so it was here earlier than the deer. Maybe a few days ago, or even a week..."

"Forget it!" Ken walked on, following Sheera, who was not interested in a scatology lesson either.

"Humph," Anneke mumbled. "You can learn a lot of important information from studying animal signs in the wild."

Ken stopped at a small stream that ran down a mossy bank. By a big rock he bent over, scooped up a handful of water, and drank it. Anneke joined him, saying nothing about the animal droppings or the chance that the water wasn't clean enough to drink and might give them an illness called beaver fever.

Soon they moved uphill again, this time with Anneke following Sheera, and Ken in the back.

"Where *is* this road?" he grumbled. "It's past 7:30! Actually, 7:33 and a half. If I hadn't given in to you and your noodle-brained ideas I could have had a snack at the Wild Rose instead." He panted heavily as he hurried on, with Sheera setting a fast pace. "I'd be home by now, relaxing, eating Mom's home-made banana bread and—"

"Oh, dry up," Anneke sighed. "Save your breath for walking."

They kept following Sheera, first on a track that curved to the right, then on a fairly steep section. Ken puffed, "I have to stop for a minute."

While they rested on a fallen log, Anneke, for the first time, allowed a big worry, like a dark shadow, to sneak into her head. What if night fell and they hadn't been found? She herself had spent many nights out in the woods, and even though Larry wasn't here, she had Sheera. But what about Ken? He had told her this morning that he hadn't liked sleeping in a tent nearly as much as curling up in his own soft bed with a good book. And here they had nothing: no beds, no warm clothes, no food, no matches even. Anneke knew it was possible to make a fire without matches, but that could take hours of rubbing sticks together. She and Larry had tried once, for fun, but had given up.

CHAPTER 9

Looking around her, Anneke also noticed that the woods were beginning to get darker. Night was falling in the mountains. It came earlier here, she knew; the sun would have gone behind the tall peaks several hours ago.

"Kenichi," she started, not quite knowing how to tell her friend, "we might not eat for a while."

"I know," he said. "I'm really hungry, too."

Anneke said, "We might not get supper at all."

"What do you mean?" His eyes got bigger. "Let's keep going." He jumped up.

Anneke stayed on the log. "Sit down," she said. "We might not be found until tomorrow. They'll be out looking for us by now. But we didn't stay where we were lost. We should have!" She slapped her own forehead. "Larry is going to be *furious* when he finds out that we wandered away. I should have known better."

"We can't stay *here*," Ken said. "There's nothing, just trees and wild animals. Did you see any wolf

84

stuff? You know, when you were studying it?"

"Wolf poop? No. And I've seen no signs of bear activity either. I looked. That poor little cub! She's even hungrier than us, I bet. And I was going to look after her. So much for her being lucky."

"What are we going to do?" Ken sounded frantic.

Anneke knew that no matter how bad she felt about their situation, she needed to keep her head clear, so she could think. So she could keep Ken calm, too. "Let's find a place with soft moss," she suggested. "And maybe branches that can be a roof, sort of. You can try making a fire by rubbing sticks together."

Ken nodded. "I saw a show about that on TV," he said. "I'll need some really dry stuff. Larry and Darryl will see our fire."

They walked on, Ken collecting bits of dry wood, Anneke looking for a safe place to sleep. Suddenly she sucked her breath in sharply. "Look!"

Ken jumped up from breaking a twig in half. "What? Oh, a cabin. Oh man. Let's go. Somebody might be home." He started towards the old log structure.

"Wait," Anneke said, softly calling her dog to her side. "We should check it out first."

"Why?"

"Just in case. You keep Sheera here beside you."

"You said something about a haunted cabin earlier," Ken said. "Did you mean this one?"

"I was just kidding," Anneke shrugged.

Slowly she walked forward, all her senses alert, her feet treading carefully to avoid twigs. Nothing moved around the cabin. No sounds came from the area.

Ever so gently she stepped ahead. *Scrunch* came a noise from close by. She froze, one foot up in the air. Something rustled right behind her. Slowly, carefully, she turned, ready to duck or run, her hands balled into fists, the word "Sheera" on the edge of her lips.

A small animal's brown hind end scurried under some brambles, a rabbit perhaps, or a marmot. Anneke let out a big breath and lowered herself to her hands and knees. She crept on behind a huge, decaying log until she was right beside the cabin. Moving around to the front, she saw a door. It was closed. A heavy chain and padlock barred the entrance.

Walking up to one of the two dirty windows, Anneke peeked in. She knocked on the glass. Nothing moved.

"OK," she called. "Nobody is here."

Ken came up beside her and together they stared into the dark interior. "Too bad it's locked," he said. "We would be a lot safer in there than out here."

"Maybe," Anneke said. "I bet it smells all musty in there. There'll probably be mice and other little critters. And the roof might not be safe anymore. It's pretty old. I wonder why the door is locked."

"So nobody steals their stuff," Ken said.

But Anneke shook her head. "There's probably nothing to steal. Usually old prospectors' cabins like these are left unlocked so people can use them. In the olden days lots of guys built cabins around here when they were looking for silver. Mostly nowadays there's nothing much in them. Except maybe matches. And there may be bunks to sleep on. I wonder if Larry knows about this one." Then a thought struck her. "If there's a cabin, there's usually a creek, for drinking water. And a trail out of here. But the path may be pretty overgrown by now."

"So what do we do? It's getting really dark." Ken's voice had that catch in it again.

"Maybe we should stay here. Let's see if there's water." Anneke looked around and sure enough, a short trail led to a bubbling stream. They had a drink and returned to the cabin.

"You keep working on making a fire. I'll see if I can figure out how to get inside."

Ken went back to collecting dry twigs and bits of moss.

"Get lots," Anneke told him. With Sheera sniffing furiously beside her, she tried opening the door. She had no luck. The wood was strong; the metal chain and lock even stronger.

Trying both of the windows, she noticed that one of the old wooden frames was cracked, and partly rotten. If only she had her tool kit, she'd be inside already. Using her Swiss Army knife, Anneke picked away at the soft, moldy wood. Soon the glass pane started to wobble. Then it fell into the cabin, breaking on the floor.

Ken came running while Anneke hoisted herself up. Soon she was inside.

"What's in there?" came her friend's anxious voice.

"It's dark. Give me a minute. And it's musty, like I told you it would be. *Ahhh!*" she squealed.

"What?" Ken yelled.

Sheera barked loudly, protectively.

"A mouse or something ran across my foot. Or, no, maybe it's a spider's web." Calming herself, realizing she was probably scaring Ken needlessly, she stood for a moment to find her bearings. After her eyes had adjusted, she inspected the interior, trying not to step on the pieces of glass on the dirt floor.

Along one wall, under the second window, stood a bunk bed without a mattress. That was as she had expected. The next wall had the door in it. The wall with the window she had climbed through also had a hole with a stovepipe stuck in it. The pipe hung empty, the stove gone. That was the animal highway in and out of here, she figured.

Along the last wall stood a built-in counter. Leaning close over it, Anneke scanned the top for anything useful: cans of food, matches, paper, a flashlight. No luck.

Under the counter was a shelf that was even darker than the rest of the cabin. Anneke looked at it and could make out some shapes, but couldn't tell what the objects were. Taking a deep, brave breath, she reached towards a dark object and felt it quickly, her fingertips barely touching it. A glass jar. Yes, she was sure that's what it felt like. Taking the object from the shelf, she carried it to the window. It *was* a glass jar. And she could have kissed it, in spite of the filth, because inside, like beacons in the night, lay a handful of matches.

Would they still work? Try as she might, Anneke couldn't open the lid. "Ken," she called. "Matches. Here, open the jar." She handed the glass container out.

"Do they work?" she called after a few seconds.

"Just a minute. The lid is stuck," came the answer.

Anneke waited until she heard the sound of breaking glass.

"What do I strike them on?" Ken asked.

"Give me one." Excitedly Anneke held out her hand. She felt Ken drop some matches onto her palm. Clutching the rest like a treasure, she took one and struck it against the rough metal ring that held the stovepipe to the wall. Nothing happened. She struck again, quickly, sharply. No light.

Taking another match, she tried again, striking once, twice, three times. "Yes," she said, as the sudden hiss of a flame lit the cabin.

Carefully protecting the match from any draft, she walked to the shelf under the counter. The first thing she found, standing right beside where the jar of matches had been, was a candle in a holder. She lit the wick.

"Ken," she called, "I've got a light. And there's something here on the shelf that's...Oh." She caught her breath and stared. There, behind cobwebs and bits of paper that small rodents had chewed on, lay a little carving. Anneke held the candle as close as she dared, not wanting to set the bits of paper on fire.

She reached out and carefully took the red wooden object, rubbed it against her shorts, and held it up in the light. Yes, it was a carving like the one she had found in the river. Putting the candle down on the counter, she took Hotei from her pocket and placed the two carvings side by side. They were different gods, but the same size and made from the same wood. Carved by the same person, Anneke was sure. This had to be another of the missing netsuke Ken's mom was looking for.

"What are you doing?" she heard her friend say. "It's really dark now."

"I got us a way back into your mom's good books," she said. "You'll never believe what I found."

"What? Food?"

"No, way better than food. Another one of those missing carvings. I'm sure it's one from your mom's set. It's the one she showed me in the book, the god that has a fat belly and a sack of rice over his shoulder and a rat sitting on his foot. I can't remember his name."

"Big deal," she heard her friend mumble.

"But Ken, your mom will forget to be furious with us when she sees this. It's beautiful. Here." She handed him the god through the window frame.

Ken took the carving but said, "It's too dark."

"Just a minute." Anneke quickly searched the rest of the shelf and found nothing of value other than some cans of baked beans. Taking one of the cans and a handful of paper bits, she went back to the window and handed the candle and the food to Ken. "Protect the flame from any wind," she said. "We'll build a small fire."

"Big fire," he said.

"Small," Anneke said, hanging half in, half out of the window frame. "There's actually a ban on open fires." She jumped down to the ground. "It's too dry. There's hardly any wind, but we don't want to start a forest fire."

"That'll make them come and get us," Ken said.

Anneke hoped he was joking; he sounded so surly, she wasn't sure. Noticing the miserable look on her friend's face she said, "Don't worry, Kenichi. We'll be found. I *know* Larry is searching for us by now. He may be here sooner than you think."

"That's why we need a big fire," Ken said. "So they know we're on *this* side of that stupid river."

"No, we can't risk it." Anneke took the second carved god back from Ken and slid it into her other pocket. Scooping the bits of mice-shredded paper up from the windowsill, she looked for the safest place to build a little fire. It had to be away from dry moss, needles, and grasses, away from tree roots and overhanging branches. "Let's get some rocks," she said.

They built a small makeshift firepit by encouraging Sheera to dig a hole, which they lined with rocks.

"One more rock," Anneke said, scanning her surroundings.

"I think that's good enough for...Ahhh!" Ken shot up onto his feet as a loud "hoo, hoo-hoo, hoo-hoo" came from above them. "What's..."

"Shhh," Anneke whispered. "That's a great horned owl. There's one around our place some-times too. It's probably checking you out to see if you would make a tasty midnight snack."

Ken muttered something and peered into the surrounding darkness.

"I was kidding," Anneke whispered quickly. "Great horned owls only eat small stuff, like rabbits and mice."

"I know that," Ken snapped back. "I'm not stupid. I do read books, you know."

"Great horned owls are beautiful big birds," Anneke said, ignoring Ken's mood. "I love their huge, yellow, staring eyes. I saw one once, with Larry. I wish we had a flashlight. Then you could see it."

Ken sat down. "I hate this," he said miserably. "I just want to be back home."

"I'm really, really sorry," Anneke said. "We'll be fine though. We will! Let's start the fire and heat the can of beans."

Ken held the candle to the bits of paper and twigs in the pit.

"Good," Anneke said. "That'll keep everything away."

"What do you mean by everything?"

Anneke tried to sound light and unworried. She decided not to use the word "bear" again. "Oh, squirrels, rabbits, you know. And besides, Sheera would sniff out and scare off whatever comes too close."

"Could we sleep in there?" Ken pointed to the cabin.

"You could," Anneke said. "There's one bunk."

Ken looked at the open window, back at the fire, then at Sheera, who had snuggled in between them. "I'll stay here for now," he decided.

CHAPTER 10

While Ken put more sticks on the fire and grumbled about the lack of plates and forks, Anneke worked at opening the beans with the can opener on her Swiss Army knife. She realized that, to keep her friend calm, she needed to distract him from their situation. What would Larry do? Tell a story or a joke. After she managed to get the lid open, she put the can on one of the rocks beside the fire. "We'll eat soon," she said. "This could be Grubby Graeme's cabin."

"Who's Grubby Graeme?"

"Larry told us a story when we went on a picnic with Mother last week. He made it up for Elishia." Anneke relayed the story to Ken. By the time she was finished, the beans were hot enough to eat. Anneke found two flat pieces of wood and they took turns scooping some slippery beans from the can into their mouths.

"I feel like Grubby Graeme myself," Ken said.

"It's a good thing my mom can't see me eat like this." Just then a bean slid off the wood and onto his shirt. He didn't notice it. Anneke said nothing.

"I could eat another whole can full," Ken said when they'd finished.

"There's more." Anneke got up, glad to see that her friend was beginning to feel better. "I'll get three cans. One for Sheera too." She lighted the candle with a burning twig.

When they had each finished another can, Anneke said, "Gram says she makes the best baked beans, but I don't know."

"These cans looked pretty new still. Do you think someone brought them here not too long ago?" Ken asked.

Anneke nodded. "No rust on the cans," she said. "I checked them. The way Larry showed me."

"You're lucky to have Larry," Ken said. "You know everything. If I did, I wouldn't worry so much about getting lost either."

"I'm worried all right. He's *really* going to be mad at me. He'll tell me I should know better."

"Maybe," Ken said. "But he'd be cool for a dad."

"So would Darryl," Anneke said. "He's pretty cool too. I bet he'd get along great with Larry. Darryl and Larry and you and me could go camping. Sometimes I wish Larry wasn't married. Maybe he and my mother... No, I guess not."

They sat in silence for a while before Anneke said, "Sometimes I think it would be nice just to have a normal family. Sometimes I think I will let

94

them adopt me. But what about Mother. She'd be as lonely as that crying cub. I can't..."

After another long silence, Ken said, "Larry and Eileen are so normal together." When Anneke gave him a dirty look he quickly added, "I didn't mean your mom...I mean *my* mom and Darryl are so different."

"So are Larry and Eileen. So are Eileen and my mother. When my mother has a good day...and Eileen wants to treat me like a four-year-old...and Larry tells me stuff in front of Eileen, I feel...I don't know." Shaking her head, she watched a little red flame slowly creep up a stick. The stick would soon be burning all over and become ashes. It would never be wood again. Jumping up, Anneke grabbed the four empty bean cans. "I'll get some water to put beside the fire. Just to be sure. I'll be right back."

When she returned, each can half full of water, her T-shirt and arms soaked, she sat closer to the heat of the flames and took both gods from her pocket again. "I wonder why this netsuke was in the cabin," she said. "Could your grandparents' relatives have lived here?"

"Was it really messy in there?" Ken asked.

"Yes. But mostly it was empty."

"They wouldn't have been my relatives then," Ken said, curling his bare arms around his chest.

"But when they left the Internment Camp they were probably really poor. So maybe they built this cabin," Anneke speculated. "Back then it would have looked nice and new."

"I doubt it," Ken said. "Why wouldn't my grandparents have known where those relatives were? This is probably a different netsuke."

"It's from the same set." Anneke wanted to be right. "It has to be. I bet I solved your mom's problem."

Ken shrugged. "I'm still majorly going to get it this time."

"So am I." Anneke scratched a mosquito bite on her ankle. "I wonder, though, if it was them, your relatives I mean, and they were poor, why didn't they sell the netsuke? Why was one here in an abandoned cabin, and one in the river? And where is the seventh netsuke? Your mom said these things were worth a lot of money." She put the two gods back in her pockets.

Ken yawned noisily. "Tomorrow," he said, stretching, "as soon as it's light, we'll find that road. Right now I'll keep the fire going." He threw a few more sticks on the small flames.

Anneke yawned too. "Tomorrow I want to find the cub again. I keep thinking of her. She's so little. She won't survive alone. I guess you didn't hear her crying the way I did. I can't get rid of that sad sound in my head."

Yawning again, Anneke pointed to the two flat places on the ground and said, "You sleep here, I sleep there." Exhausted from the long day's events, she lay down.

Something cuddled up against Anneke's chest. She curled her arms around the furry black body of her dog. No, it wasn't Sheera, it was the bear cub. The little one licked her chin, the way Sheera usually did when the two of them had an especially cozy snuggle together.

"You can both be my favourite pets," she said. "Loving one of you doesn't mean I can't love the other at the same time."

Snap, crackle.

Anneke struggled out of her sleep. She opened her eyes, sat up, and looked around in surprise. Oh yes, they were sleeping out here by the cabin in the woods. Ken was putting another stick on the fire. The twigs that were already burning snapped and crackled loudly. The flames danced crazily. Sheera lay beside Ken, her head on his leg. The tree trunks directly surrounding the camp stood tall and steady like silent guards in the fire's light. Behind and above her, the forest loomed darkly in its nighttime stillness. A lone coyote called for company.

I hate this," Ken mumbled, moving even closer to the fire.

"That coyote is a long way off," Anneke told him.

"There's a lot of them," he said.

"No, just one. A coyote can make a call that sounds like there's a group of them, all answering each other."

Ken didn't look like he believed her. He shivered. "I'm cold." He put another two sticks on the fire.

"Don't start a forest fire," Anneke mumbled before she felt herself drifting off into sleep once more.

When the first birds started singing, Anneke

woke up again. With her eyes still closed, she guessed at the sounds. She thought the loud screeching was made by a Steller's Jay, while she could also hear the chick-a-dee-dee-dee call of the bird that said its own name. She opened her eyes and searched the trees. She was right about the chickadee, but the screeching came from a big black raven who, perched on a low branch not far away, was trying to tease Sheera into a game of chase. The dog ignored the dare and, full of her own importance, continued to guard the kids by the fire.

Ken lay curled up by the ashes, his hands tucked under his cheek like a little pillow. His eyes were closed. Anneke whispered his name, but there was no response. Only the dog looked at her. Anneke's eyes closed again too, and she slid back into sleep.

The next time she woke, she heard Ken yawn loudly and walk around. "Good girl," he told Sheera. Anneke sat up.

"The fire went out," he said. "I tried to keep it going. There are lots of wild animals around here. I didn't sleep at all."

Anneke grinned. "Congratulations. You spent your first night right out in the woods."

Ken scowled and muttered. "I was cold." He rubbed his bare arms, which showed goosebumps. "And that ground is as hard as a rock."

"From now on, sleeping in a sleeping bag, on a foamy, in a tent will be extra comfy." Anneke stood up, feeling stiff. "Move your arms and legs around," she said.

They stood in a small, open, sunny patch and jogged on the spot. "Breakfast would be nice," Ken said.

"More beans?" Anneke asked. "There's one can left." When Ken nodded, she went back into the cabin. There was a little more light this time, but Anneke saw nothing else on the shelf that interested her, no third netsuke.

They decided to eat the beans cold and have a very short search for the road. "We won't go far," Anneke stressed. "We'll come back here."

They walked uphill a little, staying close enough that Anneke knew they could find the cabin again. The trees were thick. There was no road, no sound of traffic, no rushing river water.

After they returned to the cabin, Anneke said, "Let's try that trail that goes to the creek. It crosses and goes on from there. As long as it doesn't branch off, we'll be able to find our way back here."

"We could leave a note," Ken suggested.

"*Great* idea." Anneke hoped her friend would stay in a good mood until they were found. They *would* be found soon, now that it was light. At any minute Anneke expected to hear Larry's familiar call of "Yoohoo?" bounce off the silent trees.

With a pointy stick and mud they printed the words *Ken, Anneke, here* on the back of the label from the bean can. They left the white label weighted down with a rock in front of the door.

CHAPTER 11

At the creek, Sheera had a morning swim of sorts, crawling on her belly up and down in the water. Then, before Anneke managed to get far enough away, the dog shook herself, spraying water around her.

Muttering, Anneke wiped her soaked legs before she hurried after Ken.

"Look at this," he called out, standing at the edge of a steep cliff. "Man, that is a *long* way down." Cautiously, he crawled on his stomach to the very edge and peered over it.

Anneke came up beside him and dropped a pebble. They watched as it fell straight, then bounced off some ledges and into the trees far below. "This is *not* the way to go," she said.

"No," Ken said excitedly. "But listen."

In the distance, down below somewhere, they could hear the faint rushing of water.

"The river," Anneke exclaimed.

Scrambling back from the edge a little, Ken said, "We want to go down there. But how?"

"We stay up here," Anneke decided.

Ken nodded. "I can see water glistening over there though." He pointed to the left and down. "If we stay close enough to the edge, we won't get lost. Let's search along here. We might find a trail to the river."

They moved on, staying away from the drop-off. Ken was in front again. Suddenly he stopped and turned his head, his finger across his lips. He pointed with his other hand. Anneke nodded. She'd already seen it too. A little ways ahead of them, in a small clearing not very far from the cliff's edge, lay a wildcat.

Silently Anneke backed up to where Sheera was sniffing at a small hole under a tree root. Taking the dog by the collar, she whispered sharply, "Listen to me. Be quiet." Cautiously, with a firm grip on her dog, she walked forward until she could see the cat. She kneeled and made Sheera, who was still looking back at the animal hole, lie down beside her.

The wildcat basked lazily in the morning sun, her paws up in the air, her belly exposed. The beautiful reddish-brown mottled fur shone, while her ears, small and tufted, were clearly visible. Was that a bobcat or a lynx? Anneke wondered.

Before she had time to ponder the question, two kittens tumbled out of the shrubs behind the cat. Mewing, they pounced up to the mother cat and started suckling. Their little furry bodies were still for a few minutes while they drank their mother's milk.

Sheera's muscles tensed. Her eyes stared at the three animals. Anneke put her hand around her dog's muzzle as she and Ken grinned at each other and watched as first one, and then the second kitten scooted back to the shrubs. They chased each other around a tree trunk before, quick as a flash, one scrambled up. The little rear-end, short stubby tail and all, disappeared behind a branch.

But just as quickly the kitten reappeared, hanging from the branch by its front paws, its lithe body swinging back and forth like a pendulum. Big, round, curious kitten eyes looked down at the other cats. The second kitten climbed up the trunk a little way, jumped down again, did a somersault, body round as a ball, and ran to its mother. The female stayed stretched out in the sun, ignoring the pouncing kitten. Only when the little one bit her face did she swipe a lazy paw at her naughty child. The kitten mewed and scooted up the tree in search of its playmate. No sooner had it disappeared than both came tumbling back down, scampering and jumping, mewing and pouncing. They chased a dead leaf as if it were an escaping mouse. Next they played hide-and-seek around and over their mother's body until finally the adult gave a fierce grumble.

Sheera whimpered. "Shhh," Anneke hissed. But it was too late. The protective mother had heard the sounds and, suddenly fully awake, she called her kittens to her and hurried them to the edge of the cliff. For a fraction of a second the three animals froze there in a ready-to-pounce stance, front paws a little over the edge already, rear-ends up in the air. Then the mother cat jumped and was gone from view. The kittens followed.

Anneke, Sheera, and Ken rushed to the edge of the cliff, but when they got there, they stopped. Anneke dropped onto her hands and knees. Sheera whimpered. Ken lay down.

"That is steep," he said.

"Fine for them I guess." Anneke looked wistfully at the three flexible cats as, lower down, they jumped from one skinny ledge to another. Soon the animals ran into the trees below and disappeared from view.

"That was so cool," Ken said. "They played just like regular kittens."

"They *are* cats," Anneke said. "Wildcats. Either bobcats or lynx."

"I know that!" Ken sat up, away from the cliff edge. "They are felines, belonging to the same group as cougars, lions, leopards, and house cats. They are all carnivores."

Anneke rolled her eyes. Ken and his fancy words. "They all drink mother's milk and they are cute and quick and they have sharp claws," she added her bit of wisdom.

"Yes, they are mammals. And they have retractable claws," he said.

Anneke shrugged. Give it up, she thought.

"I've never watched them at play like that before," Ken said. "Only on TV."

Anneke nodded. "Larry and I saw a bobcat in the woods once at night. They're nocturnal animals. I wonder why they were out in the sun today. I'm glad Sheera was so quiet. Good girl."

"Let's keep going." Ken got up. "Maybe the cliff's less steep farther along."

Anneke scrambled to her feet as well. "Not too far," she said. "We can't just keep walking and walking. Larry will be at the cabin soon."

Ken nodded. "Just a bit more."

Only a minute or two later, though, the edge started sloping downward, and the cliff became less of a sheer drop.

"Great," Ken said. "This is better. We're going in the right direction. The river is down there some-where. I can see water glistening." He sent a pebble over the edge and it rolled along the slope rather than dropping straight down.

They walked on, but suddenly found themselves in shrubs and trees growing thickly right up to the edge of the drop-off. It seemed impossible to move on.

"I'm ready to give up," Ken said in disgust. "Let's go back." He wiped his sweaty forehead with his shirt.

But Anneke, who had rounded a clump of greenery, caught a glimpse of a different colour glimmering through some thin trees. She took another two steps and stopped.

"Ken," she called. "Come here. Look!"

He came quickly. Together they stared at the steep mountains rising up on the other side of a turquoise lake. Here and there, ribbons of yellow sand separated the blue water and the green trees. Between the mountains ran deep, narrow gullies down which waterfalls crashed. High atop the peaks, white snow glistened in the morning sun.

"New Denver Glacier," Anneke said.

"Cool. I don't think I've ever been this high up." Ken stared across the valley. "That icefield looks big from up here," he said. "I wish I could fly over it."

Anneke squinted. "I wish I had my sunglasses," she said. Then slowly she added, "You know...the river we crossed...well...it runs into that lake. It's Slocan Lake. We're *way* too high. And *way* too far along. We'll *never* get there from here. And if people are looking for us, they'll never look here. We need to go back right away."

Ken agreed. "But don't you think there might be a way to..." He stopped and they both looked in the direction of a sound. "What..." he started.

"That's the noise of a helicopter," Anneke yelled. "Come on. Let's get back into an open space. They're looking for us."

"Over there," Ken pointed. "Where we were a few minutes ago. Where I rolled that pebble down the slope. There's that big open spot. Let's go."

Sheera barked and led the way as they hurried back along the slope, over a few rocks and logs, through some shrubs, and to an open area right along the cliff. From here, a different part of the valley was visible; the New Denver Glacier was gone and the helicopter's sound was more faint. But then the chopper came around the bend and into full view, its blue-and-white body moving along above the lake like a remote-control toy.

"Here we are," Ken yelled, jumping up and down.

"Use your red-and-yellow shirt as a flag," Anneke called to him. "Here we are, here." She ran back and forth, waving her arms frantically. Sheera barked and barked, happy finally to be allowed to make lots of noise.

Ken, flapping his shirt through the air above his head, was frantically jumping up and down. One of his feet landed on a loose shelf of rock and he lost his balance, his shirt falling over his head, blocking his vision. He grabbed for a tree stump, but his hand missed. He tried to pull the shirt from his eyes, but the cloth stayed over his face. Blindfolded, panicked, he teetered for a second. His feet slipped. They loosened more rocks that tumbled down the slope. Ken cried out, and like a piece of broken rock he joined the crumbling edge in a mad downward rush.

Anneke snatched for his arm, his hand, his hair even. She missed. Horrified, she watched as her friend, lying on his side, careened down the steep slope. Bits of loose debris rolled and bounced all around him. His shirt, like a colourful marker, clung to a rock on the path he made as he slid, down, down, picking up more speed as he went.

"A tree. To the left," Anneke yelled. "Grab it if..." But even as she called out, Ken continued on past the tree, missing it narrowly. She saw him flailing his arms and legs, straining to get a hold of something, anything, to slow himself down. He clutched at a rocky ledge with one hand, bringing his slide to a sudden, jerky halt. He dangled there by one arm, his feet feeling for something to stand on, but finding no ledges. His other hand groped for a bigger, better hold, with no luck.

A second went by. Another second. Sheera whimpered. "Stay," Anneke whispered, willing Ken to find a better, more solid grip. Wanting him to climb all the way back up. Knowing he couldn't.

As his feet searched for a ledge to stand on, as his free hand felt the steep slope's surface for support, any small irregularity—a rock that wasn't loose, a bump he could grab, or a hole he could wedge his fingers into—Anneke held her breath. Helplessly, she watched in horror as slowly, slowly his fingers started to slip. As his hand lost its grip. As he again started sliding.

A little lower his feet hit a tiny ledge, but instead of breaking his fall, the ledge flipped him head over heals so that this time he landed on his bare back and continued that way, his legs and feet up in the air.

"*Watch out!*" she screamed. "Ahhh!" She winced as she saw her friend smack into a lone tree growing on a ledge.

All movement stopped.

"Ken? Are you OK? Kenichi? Say something."

No answer. The body lay in a heap at the base of the tree far below. Anneke scanned the slope.

Could she climb down? No, the only way from here would be the way he had gone.

"Ken!" she yelled as loudly as she could, her hands cupped around her mouth. No response. Anneke searched the sky. No sign of the chopper anywhere. In the distance she could hear the machine's whirring blades, the sound bouncing and echoing through the valley like a far-off drum roll gone wild.

"They never even saw us." Scrambling to her feet, Anneke backed away from the edge. What am I going to do? she thought, frantically looking farther along the ridge for a way down. But the drop from the edge was even steeper in other places.

"Ken," she called again. "Kenichi, move. *Please!*" In the vastness of the valley at her feet, the last word sounded like the final dying wail of a siren.

Sheera, unsettled by her owner's loud cry, rushed to her side.

"Oh pup, should I leave? Go back to the cabin? Wait for the chopper?"

Sheera started running back and forth along the edge, looking at Anneke, at Ken, at the steep drop. She whimpered.

"You go down," Anneke urged. She had seen Sheera cover some very steep terrain. The dog might be able to get to Ken without falling. But then what? Ken still hadn't moved. "Go on, find Ken," Anneke coaxed. Puzzled, Sheera pressed against her. She didn't go down the slope.

"Kenichi," Anneke called once more. "Ken, answer me!" No response. Her friend lay completely still.

CHAPTER 12

I have to get help, Anneke decided. I need to find a way out of here...

She watched with shock as her pet took off at top speed. Was she giving chase to a wild animal? "Not now, Sheera. Come back."

The dog barked. She rushed back to her owner, then ran away again. Anneke looked up and there, in the direction they had come from, was another dog on a leash—a big black Lab, held by a short, dark-haired man in khaki clothes. Behind him came a woman in jeans and a T-shirt. She was tall, with curly blond hair. Last came Larry.

"You found us," Anneke yelled, rushing to Larry and throwing her arms around his neck. Sheera bounced forward as well, heading straight for them, taking one last flying leap to end up against Larry's legs.

"Whoa, pooch. Yes, yes, I'm happy to see you too." He laughed as the dog put her front paws against his side, wanting in on the embrace.

"Larry," Anneke called, pulling back. "Help Ken. He's there" She pointed. "He fell when we saw the helicopter, and we waved like crazy, and he lost his balance, and he slid down, and he hasn't moved, and...."

The three adults looked down, then immediately swung into action.

"We need the chopper," the short man decided, taking charge. "I have a rope here," he continued, "but it may not be long enough. Peterson," he directed the woman, "you contact the pilot. Proost," he nodded at Larry, then pointed, "you tie *this* rope end to *that* tree. Anneke, I'm Mr. Richards. You watch these two guys." He nodded briskly towards the two dogs, then said to the Lab, "Petto, sit. Stay." Taking his blue baseball cap off, he wiped his forehead.

Anneke called Sheera over and told her to sit as well. She stood between the two dogs and watched as Ms. Peterson contacted the helicopter pilot. Soon she said, "The chopper is on her way."

From his pack Mr. Richards took a climber's harness and strapped it around his body. He clipped one end of the rope to the harness while Larry secured the other end to the tree. Mr. Richards called, "Ready?" and when Larry nodded, he carefully started lowering himself down over the edge, holding the rope with both hands. Larry let out the rope while slowly, step by little step, Mr. Richards disappeared over the edge. He worked his way towards Ken.

"Kenichi!" Anneke called, looking at her friend again after watching the adults for the last few minutes. "He moved! Larry, he is lying differently from before. He's alive, he's..." The words caught and she cleared her full throat.

Just then Ken moved again. He bent one leg, then slowly pushed himself up a little on one arm.

"Stay still, boy," Mr. Richards called from halfway down the slope. "Just lie very still until I get there." He took another step, then another. When he passed Ken's shirt, he picked it up and tucked it into his belt.

"That's just about it," Larry called. "The rope's too short."

Anneke heard Mr. Richards mumble something she couldn't understand. Hanging at the end of the line, he pushed his upper body out from the cliff with his hands, scanning the slope as if he were looking for something. At the same moment the chopper came into view around the bend. Ms. Peterson started waving and the helicopter made a sharp turn, came down lower, and then headed in their direction. Anneke could see the belly of the blue-and-white machine now. The letters RCMP were clearly visible on the bottom. She felt the wind from the whirring blades. The branches of the tree Ken lay against swung wildly. Here and there, sand blew off the cliff in tiny imitation funnel clouds. She heard Ms. Peterson talking to the pilot as the machine began to hover exactly over the climber.

While the chopper hung in the air, a line with what looked like a metal ring as big as a dinner plate was lowered to the rescuer. Everyone watched in silence as the rope swung back and forth, back and forth, past Mr. Richards. It came in close, bounced off the slope, and sailed out again while the man reached as far as he could, his hand ready to grab the ring.

"Yes!" Larry said when Mr. Richards finally managed to snatch the swinging object. Anneke breathed a sigh of relief as she watched the agile climber unclip himself from the rope he had climbed down on. He grabbed the ring with both hands, gave a big nod, and the chopper pulled him up into the air a little before lowering him farther down the hillside. When he was as close to Ken as the tree branches would allow, he let go of the ring and scrambled over to the boy.

The noise of the hovering helicopter drowned out any other sound as everyone watched the man slowly examine Ken. He felt his head, his neck, his back, his legs, his elbows.

Minutes ticked away and Anneke couldn't stand still any longer. She walked back and forth, muttering, "Let him be OK, *please,* let him be fine!" If that dumb tree hadn't fallen across the river...No, if she, Anneke, hadn't been dumb enough to cross that tree, Ken wouldn't be lying there right now. But then she wouldn't have found the starving cub either. She tried to think about the cub, but her eyes kept staring at her friend, lying there so still against the tree. Her mind would not think anything except, please let Ken be fine. It's all my fault. He *has* to be OK.

Finally Mr. Richards put up his arms to give a signal.

"He's all right," Larry called, throwing his hands up to the sky as well.

"Thank God," Ms. Peterson said, her tanned face stretching into a huge smile of relief. "The poor chap. That was quite a fall."

Anneke felt herself grinning from ear to ear, unable to say a word. When Larry put an arm around her shoulder, she hugged him so hard they wobbled back and forth, almost falling against a tree trunk.

Anneke watched with fascination as a harness was lowered from the helicopter on the line. One of Ken's arms was tied against his body, he was strapped into the harness and then, slowly, slowly, with Mr. Richards beside him, they were pulled up and up on the end of the line. They hung there while the helicopter headed away from the cliff.

Everyone watched until the chopper had disappeared around a bend.

"Lucky," she mumbled. "He gets to ride out."

"He'll be plenty sore," Ms. Peterson said. "I wouldn't be surprised if they fly him straight to the hospital."

"Hanging there like that?" Larry asked.

"No, they'll set down on a flat part and put him on a stretcher, I'm sure," Ms. Peterson said.

"But I thought Mr. Richards gave a sign that he was all right," Anneke's good feelings collapsed.

"Sure. As in nothing is too serious or life-threatening," Ms. Peterson said.

"He'll be scraped and bruised," Larry added.

"And unless he's really lucky, probably quite a bit worse than just a few bruises."

"I'm sure glad you found us," Anneke said. "I didn't know what to do. I was really getting frantic."

"*You* were getting frantic! How do you think Mrs. Uno feels? And the others? How on earth did you two end up all the way over here in the first place?" Larry asked, his face becoming a dark cloud, his voice switching from concern to anger.

"We got lost. There's this baby bear up a tree, and after Sheera lost the smell because of a deer we were lost and..." Anneke's words came rushing out like rocks that had wobbled on the edge of a cliff for too long. Finally she ended the whole story with, "How did you find the cabin?"

"Petto's nose," Larry said. "He's Mr. Richards' search-and-rescue dog. By the way, Ms. Peterson here is with the local search and rescue as well."

"We knew about the cabin," Ms. Peterson said. "It was used for illegal activities, so we had to lock it. Did you push the window in, or was it like that when you found it last night?"

"I did that. And guess what I found inside." Remembering the second netsuke, Anneke pulled both carvings from her pockets.

"That's interesting," Ms. Peterson said, frowning. "The other two missing ones."

"Yes," Larry put in, a strange, concerned look on his face. "Mr. Richards, found one of these carvings in the cabin as well this morning. Actually, Petto sniffed it out. Mr. Richards knows someone in the valley, a Mr. Onoda. He used to have three of them, but someone broke into his house and stole them all."

"Somebody stole the netsuke?" Anneke looked puzzled. "And Mr. Richards knows the relatives?" She shook her head in disbelief.

"You have two of the three stolen netsuke," Larry said, frowning. "How did you get them? How did you know one was in that cabin? How could another one ever have been in the river on a sandbar? And why did Petto, who was sniffing out *your* scent, lead us to the third stolen netsuke?"

Larry looked at her with great concern, Anneke noticed. Then a thought struck her. Incredulously she asked, "You don't think *I* stole these netsuke, do you?"

"I don't know." Larry looked like he wasn't sure what to believe. "You came up to the cabin where two of these were hidden. And you tried to hide the other carving from us at home."

"I did not!" Anneke started.

But Larry held up his hand. "Mr. Richards' friend and I will talk to you about all of this. But we'll wait until we get safely back home."

Safely back home, Anneke thought. They don't even believe me.

"So tell me, why didn't you stay put if you were lost?" Larry asked. "The number of times I've told you to stay in one place and let people *find* you."

"I know. I first got lost because of the cub. And then it just went on from there."

"You've mentioned a cub twice now," Ms.

Peterson said. "What cub?"

"There's a tiny cub. I saw her. She's up a tree somewhere close to the river, all alone and starving."

Larry groaned. "Of all the things I taught you," he said, shaking his head and looking discouraged. "A cub means a sow is in the area."

"No," Anneke said. "There's no mother bear."

"She could be right," Ms. Peterson said. "There has been some poaching going on around here. That's partly why the cabin is locked. We should at least check it out. I'll notify the conservation office in Nelson."

Anneke nodded. She had finally done something right. The little one would be found. The cub would be safe, as long as she was still in that tree.

Ms. Peterson contacted the chopper pilot again, then patted Anneke on her shoulder and said, "We'll find the cub, I'm sure."

"I called her Lucky," Anneke said. "but she'll be starving. I hope she's still alive."

"Let's head up to the road," Ms. Peterson said.

Petto didn't want to leave the cliff's edge. His owner had told him to stay, so he wasn't going to move.

"It's OK," Larry said, petting the shiny black head. "Come on, your owner is already down in the valley."

But Petto didn't budge, so Ms. Peterson put a rope on him and pulled while Larry nudged and encouraged the Lab along beside him. The dog kept looking back and hesitating for quite a while.

"He's such a well-trained animal," Ms. Peterson said.

"Like Sheera," Larry said. "She really listens too."

Anneke followed her pet, thinking Larry sounded less angry already. They found a partly overgrown, steep, narrow animal track that led up the hill. Anneke hadn't seen the track; she and Ken had gone in the wrong direction that morning.

"I feel like a mountain goat," Larry commented at one point as they clambered along a skinny ledge. "It's a good thing we're all experienced hikers."

Anneke thought about the mother wildcat and her kittens jumping from foothold to foothold like bouncing balls. She'd tell Larry and the others what they'd seen. She especially wanted to tell Elishia. But for the moment she needed to concentrate on putting her feet in the right places.

When they were safely on the gravel road Anneke had tried to find the previous night, they walked down it until Mr. Richards met them with his truck. He stopped and jumped out when he saw them.

"How's Ken?" everyone asked at once.

"He's gone on to the hospital," Mr. Richards said. "Whoa, Petto, whoa," he laughed as his dog bounded over and greeted him so joyfully he almost knocked his owner to the ground.

"Ken will be fine," he continued. "He was lucky. He may have a broken arm though, and he has lots of cuts and bruises. His mom and Darryl are with him now, so I thought I'd come up here and give you a ride back to your vehicles."

CHAPTER 13

They drove to Rosebery, where they waited for the conservation officer. While the adults talked about search and rescue, Anneke threw sticks for Sheera and Petto, staying as far out of the way as she could. She wished she were invisible; she would be facing Larry once he finished talking to the adults. Miserably, she listened to them discussing how expensive it was to send for the search-and-rescue helicopter.

Another man joined them after a while. "Hello, John," Ms. Peterson called. She introduced the man as John Parker, the conservation cfficer, and added, "He'll help us find the cub. He's an expert on bears." Ms. Peterson told him Anneke's story about the cub in the tree.

Mr. Parker suggested they leave the dogs in the trucks. In single file, with the conservation officer in the front, followed by Anneke, Larry, Ms. Peterson, and Mr. Richards, they made their way to the fallen tree across the river.

Mr. Parker looked concerned when he saw the makeshift bridge, his dark, bushy eyebrows coming together at the crease above his sunburnt nose. He tied a rope to a tree close to the log and insisted that he go across first to tie the rope to a tree on the other side as well. Then he told everyone to hold onto the rope while they crossed. "This water is far too wild," he said. "If someone falls off that slippery log they could be swept down the river."

Larry gave Anneke a look she'd rather have missed.

Once on the other side, she led them to the fallen trunk she had stood on the day before, then to the rock outcropping she had sat on when she and Sheera had heard the noise of the cub climbing up into the tree.

She pointed. "Lucky was right there."

While they moved around some shrubs, Anneke's heart gave a quick little jump when she heard the tiny cry, still as sad, as scared, as lonely as the day before, as if from a baby in distress. Excitedly she called, "Lucky's alive! I heard her."

Far above their heads, nestled on a big branch of the tree, sat the frightened cub.

"Ohhhh," Anneke whispered. "She looks so lonely."

The animal cried again, its baby snout pointing down, dark eyes looking at each person in turn.

"I'll try to lure the cub out of the tree with warm condensed milk mixed with honey," Mr. Parker said. "Bears have a very strong sense of smell. Everyone else, move way back."

Mr. Parker stayed by the pine tree with a dish of

milk, leather gloves on his hands, and a piece of leather spread out like a blanket on the ground beside him. Ms. Peterson picked up the other pair of gloves and moved the rest of the group back behind some shrubs and a big fallen tree.

Mr. Parker made little smacking and grunting sounds. The cub looked at him. She cried a few times in answer but stayed up on the branch.

Time ticked by slowly. No one moved. What would happen to the little bear? Anneke wondered. Would an orphan animal go to a foster home the way human children did?

After a while Mr. Parker called, "This isn't working. We need to get someone who can go up the tree to bring the cub down."

Everyone stood and stretched.

"I can scale the tree," Mr. Richards said. "If I get my gear from the truck."

The conservation officer decided that Mr. Richards would take Anneke and Larry across the river, get the gear, and return to the tree.

"But I want to watch," Anneke said.

"Now that we've found the cub, the fewer people the better," Mr. Parker said.

"It won't take long, once I get up there," Mr. Richards added. "Wait at the other side of the river. We'll bring the little one across."

As Anneke tried to protest again, Larry said, "It's best for the cub. The poor thing is scared of all of us."

"I guess." Anneke followed the adults.

"Leave the dogs in the truck," Mr. Parker called

after them. "It'll be better not to have them running around when we come back across the river."

Mr. Richards crossed the tree with his gear, which left only Larry and Anneke on the riverbank.

"I wonder how long they'll be," Anneke said. "I'm hungry." She thought of the Wild Rose, then shrugged. Lucky would be much hungrier.

But Larry said, "I have a sandwich and juice." He gave her his lunch. "They'll be a while, I would think. It's a bit of a job getting up a tree that tall. And the cub won't know she's being rescued. She'll try to climb up even higher, away from safety, as Mr. Richards gets closer to her."

"I wish I could watch," Anneke said. "I sort of feel that Lucky is my cub."

Larry sat down on the sand. Anneke followed his example. Neither of them spoke, and the silence stretched between them as tensely as an overtightened bow. Anneke, feeling she'd rather face Larry's anger here, without Eileen around, broke the silence. "I slept out on the hard ground. Ken did too. He hated it."

"So, are you proud of making so much trouble for your friend?" Larry snapped. "You made me a promise! I'm beginning to wonder if it was wise for Eileen and me to take you in. Especially now, with a new baby on the way."

Anneke gasped. Only last week Larry had wanted to adopt her. Now, if he'd changed his mind and he didn't want her anymore, where could she go?

"You're shocked," Larry said. "Well, it shocks me to hear myself say those words. But Anneke, I *trusted* you. You *promised* to behave on this camping trip. I took your word for that." He was yelling now. "You let me down. You let Eileen down. You let Ken down. You let his mom down. How do you think they feel? Your friend is in the hospital. His mother is worried sick. She didn't sleep all night! *None of us did!*" Larry stopped yelling and breathed deeply, obviously trying to calm himself.

"So," he finally said, "I'll be honest with you. I'm wondering if you're starting to wear us down. I don't know if I can handle your dishonesty. What it means for Elishia and the new baby."

"I always knew this would happen," Anneke said lamely. "Always Elishia, Elishia. I don't really count. The baby will need my room anyway. And if it's a boy, you'll be more interested in him—"

Larry put up his hand to stop her. "It's not about where the baby will sleep or how I will feel if it's a boy. It's about *you* and how you have behaved lately. It's about me not being able to trust you. It's about me teaching you things and then you ignoring all the lessons." Larry shook his head, then, resting his chin in one cupped hand, he mumbled, "I feel really discouraged."

"I'm not dishonest," Anneke said. "I know all the lessons you taught me. I even told Ken about lots of things."

"So," Larry said, looking up, "why do you do

these things then? And why on earth do you think you don't count? Why do you think I'd like our new baby more than you?"

"I know you like me," Anneke said. "It's just, sometimes it's like Eileen and I don't get along. I get scared that she doesn't want me around anymore."

Slowly Larry said, "If only you *really* knew. The times Eileen has changed her schedule just for you. The times she has quietly given up camping trips or hikes or even bike rides with me so you and I could go instead." He looked at Anneke sharply, a crease running across his forehead. "Before you came along, we often dropped Elishia off at Gram and Grump's to go away, just Eileen and me, for the day or an overnight. Eileen has bonded more with Elishia partly because you and I do so many things together. Actually, if you have to know the truth, *I* am the one wondering if you're too much for us. It was Eileen, early this morning, who convinced me to go along today with search and rescue to look for you. Eileen wanted to come herself, but I asked her to stay home. She hadn't slept all night. Gram and Grump weren't available to take Elishia, and because Eileen is pregnant she tires more easily. But *still* she wanted to come and find you."

They sat side by side, staring out at the same river, hearing the rush of the same water fill each of their own silences. Anneke's eyes wandered over to Larry's shorts. He was not wearing *their* shorts, nor his brown belt. He doesn't want to be my dad, she thought. She felt as if the river had sucked her under. She couldn't breathe.

Finally, when she knew for sure she would drown, right there on the dry sandbank, Larry said, still not looking at her, "Eileen was as frantic about you being lost as if Elishia had been lost." After another, shorter silence he asked, "Why do you do these things, Anneke? I don't understand. *Why?*"

Anneke wished she knew. "Just to see," she whispered.

"To see *what?* How much trouble you can get yourself into?"

"No." She shrugged. "To see the other side, I guess."

"But you made me a *promise!* Doesn't that count for anything?" Larry slowly shook his head. "You of all people *know* how cold these streams are. And how *wild.* You have so much potential, but I feel all my teaching was for nothing. And..." his face showed a big frown while his voice got louder again, "to think that there might have been a mother bear. She might have attacked you. Or Sheera. Or Ken. She could have killed all three of you."

"There was no mother bear," Anneke defended herself. "I knew that."

"No, you did *not!*" Larry's face got red. "The sow could have wandered away to get food for her cub. Think about it! A sow and her cub. And you and your dog. That is the *most* dangerous situation you could be in. And *that* you know for sure." Angrily he pounded one fist into his other hand. "Where's your brain? Honestly. This just isn't good enough.

You'll have to do better."

"I'm always looking..." Anneke started. She stopped. How could she explain the restlessness that moved around inside her, like a worm wriggling deep down in the dark? "I keep wanting to..." she started again. Then she shrugged and sighed.

They sat in silence until suddenly, surprising herself, Anneke said, "I keep thinking, or, not really thinking, but sort of feeling that I need to do something. If I do something really brave, or maybe something really daring, I'll be lucky. Mother will get better and we'll be a family again. *I want a family.* A *real* family that loves me no matter what I do." She sucked her breath in sharply. "Eileen loves me."

She looked at the river's rushing water. "Sometimes I feel..." She cleared her throat, then whispered the words quickly, very softly, as if saying them out loud might make them come true. "I feel if I love Eileen, I won't love Mother." The last word almost sounded like a sob. She cleared her throat again. "I keep wondering...Mother won't talk to me very much. Not even now that she's better. I don't know if she really *wants* me to be adopted. Why would she give me away, just like that? Especially now that she's better. She's my own mother."

Larry held a hand out to her, but he said nothing. He looked very sad, Anneke noticed.

She sat up a bit straighter. "You did come to find me." Swallowing hard, she added, "And I'm really, *really* sorry."

Gently Larry slid an arm around her shoulder. "Maybe you can talk to your mom when she's doing well. We're not sure if she and Dr. Sunnybrook would, in the end, agree to the adoption idea. That's all it was. An idea. To make you feel more like you belong. When we get home I'll phone and set up—"

"Hello! You two seem to be busy talking."

Both Anneke and Larry jumped at the sound of Mr. Richards' voice. They hadn't seen or heard anyone coming back across the tree. No one carried the bear.

"The cub. You didn't get her." Anneke's heart sank. She thought, This must be how Eileen felt last night when I didn't come home.

But then Mr. Parker's pack bulged on one side. They heard a muffled cry.

Mr. Parker put his pack down and said, "This may be a cute cub, but it's also a wild black bear in distress, with very sharp teeth and claws."

"She's a young female," Ms. Peterson said.

Of course, Anneke thought. Like me. I knew that.

When the little snout poked out of the leather blanket, Anneke couldn't help but giggle. "She's so cute. Hi, Lucky." She reached forward.

"Don't touch her," Mr. Parker warned. "Here." He handed Anneke a baby bottle. "We'll let you feed her for a minute. As a special treat."

"Oh, I can feed her as often as she needs it," Anneke said enthusiastically. "It's my summer holidays."

"She doesn't just nurse anymore," Mr. Parker

said. "She eats all kinds of other things as well: grasses, berries, fruit, insects. But a good drink of milk is still a big treat for her at this age. She's about six months old."

When Lucky smelled the bottle, she at first pushed it away with her nose. But after Mr. Parker put a little milk on his hand and rubbed it all over the nipple, Anneke tried again. This time Lucky started sucking. Happy grunting sounds came from the cub as she pulled hard on the bottle, moving Anneke's hand back and forth.

"She's strong," Larry said. "Amazing, after all that time up there in that tree."

"Yes, she'll make it," Mr. Parker said. "She's a youngster who's not only strong. She's also smart enough to adjust to a new situation. She probably came down to eat last night. But she was lonely and scared, I'm sure. We'll take her to the animal orphanage. We wondered if you'd like to come along."

"Yes," both Anneke and Larry said right away. Then Anneke added, "Could I adopt her? I could be her foster mother, sort of."

Larry squeezed her shoulder, but Mr. Parker said, "I'm sorry, but no. This cub is old and strong enough that she can be given a chance to make it in the wild. That's her own world. All she needs to stay there is a little help from someone who knows how to teach young animals to look after themselves.

CHAPTER 14

They decided that Anneke and Ms. Peterson would ride in the back of Mr. Parker's Jeep, along with Lucky. Mr. Richards went home. Larry, with Sheera, followed in his own vehicle.

All during the ride Lucky cried, grunted, and tried to get out of the knapsack. But Ms. Peterson held the cub down firmly with gloved hands.

"Could I take her home for just one day?" Anneke begged. "To show Eileen and Elishia. And," she added, feeling guilty, "Ken will want to see her."

"I'm afraid not," Mr. Parker said. "The less contact Lucky has with humans, the better it is for her. Otherwise she'll end up being a nuisance bear. That's why we fed her as little as possible. We'd have to shoot her if she became too used to people and humans' food. And we don't want to do that."

At the orphanage a woman called Mrs. Nazaroff was expecting them. "Lucky really is a lucky girl," she said. "Less than half an hour ago I got a report of a slightly injured sow with two cubs. Unfortunately one of the little ones was killed by a truck. We are going to take Lucky there."

"And try for an adoption?" Mr. Parker beamed. "Wonderful."

"Yes," Mrs. Nazaroff said. "It's a great chance for me to study the adoption of a cub by a different sow. This mother bear," she looked at Anneke again, "has a radio collar, so we can track her. We'll be able to go out and check that she has her own cub as well as Lucky with her and that she is teaching them both. But we have to be quick about it, before the sow wanders off with just the one cub. Also, I want to check her injury."

This time Anneke was told to go with Larry, while Mrs. Nazaroff rode with the other adults and Lucky.

"You can follow us to the scene," Ms. Peterson said, "but stay in your own vehicle. A wounded sow can be very dangerous. We'll get out first and tranquilize her."

Sheera greeted Anneke happily, but then she sniffed furiously and pulled back as she smelled a strange scent still on Anneke's hands. Anneke calmed her pet and gave her a big hug. "Come here, you silly mutt," she said. "Just because I love that cute little cub doesn't mean I love you less."

Along a quiet country road they stopped. During the wait and the silence in the vehicle, Anneke noticed that Larry almost nodded off twice. He hadn't slept all night, he'd said. All because of her. Anneke slid over a little closer to him.

"You can come out now, but leave the dog," Ms. Peterson called. "The mother bear is by that tree." She pointed. "We'll fix the cut to her belly."

When Anneke got to the other side of the ditch and past the shrubs, she saw Mr. Parker. He was holding the front legs of a large black bear that sat propped up against a tree as if she were a tired human having an afternoon nap. The radio collar shone around her neck like a necklace.

Mrs. Nazaroff sprayed the sow's belly. "It disinfects the wound and takes the sow's smell away," she said. "If we can get Lucky to nurse, they'll be fine. The sow will be dopey after she wakes up. With a bit of luck she won't even notice that we switched the cubs."

"How bad is her injury?" Larry asked.

"Nothing serious," Ms. Peterson said. "It'll heal."

After Mrs. Nazaroff finished stitching the wound, Mr. Parker got Lucky from the truck. "Stand well back," he said.

As Lucky wandered over to the sleeping bear, Anneke whispered, "Go on. Go to your new mother."

"There's her sister or brother," Ms. Peterson pointed. Up in a tree farther from the road sat another fluffy black ball of fur.

"You need to leave now," Mr. Parker said. "The sow may start to wake up, and we don't want her to see any of us. Mrs. Nazaroff and I will hide and watch. We'll phone you later and tell you how it ended."

"Couldn't we—" Anneke started, but Larry interrupted with, "Let's go. We've had enough of an adventure for one weekend. Everyone is waiting for us at Grump's. Gram made your favourite—baked beans and sausages."

Anneke groaned.

"Good morning," Eileen said cheerfully as she sat down on the edge of the bed.

"Morning," Anneke mumbled through a yawn. She glanced at the clock beside her bed. Eight ridiculous twenty-five! Why did Eileen have to wake her up so *early?* When it was a holiday, so there would be nothing interesting to do all day anyway. When she'd slept on the bare, hard ground the night before. Didn't this woman have more sense than... Suddenly Anneke remembered: Eileen loved her the way she loved Elishia. Anneke decided she would try harder to get along. Not sure what to say, she yawned and started a big stretch.

"Your mom wants to know if you'd like to go out for breakfast with her."

Anneke shot up into a sitting position. "Me? With Mama? Now?"

"Yes, and yes, and yes." Eileen smiled. "I knew that would get some action out of you. Elishia woke you up half an hour ago, you know."

"She did? Oh yeah, I remember, sort of." She'd fallen asleep again. She'd ignored her little sister, who had told her to get up, but not why.

Eileen put her arm around Anneke and said, "When you were lost for the night I spent some time up here, sitting on your bed, missing you. You know, this is *your* room. And it will be after the new baby is born."

"I really like it here," Anneke said.

Eileen laughed. "I didn't think I'd ever be glad to see all your clothes left all over the floor wherever they fall. Anyway, you missed your chance for a shower. Grump will be here in ten minutes. He'll drive you and your mom into Nelson."

"Ten minutes." Anneke jumped out of bed.

Only five minutes later, Eileen called up the stairs that Grump had arrived. Anneke yanked a comb through her hair and ran downstairs. Then she ran back up to get the two netsuke. She wanted to show them to Mother and tell her the whole story of the weekend. Mother would believe that Anneke had found, not stolen, the carvings. Mama knew her daughter was honest. And on good days she loved to listen to exciting stories. This sure was a good day, or they wouldn't be going into town, just the two of them, to eat at a restaurant on a Monday morning.

Feeling like singing out loud, her feet almost hovering above the steps as she rushed downstairs, she heard Eileen calling, "Have fun. Be good."

For a second Anneke almost stopped running. "Be good" was something your parents told you. She, Anneke, was going *with her parent*. As she bounced out the door, she called, "I will," and decided not to worry about anything. Hugging Sheera and telling her to stay, that she'd be back, she hopped into the waiting car.

"Hi, Grump."

"Hi, gorgeous. If you look any happier you'll start outshining the sun. Buckled up?"

At the group home Mother sat waiting on the bench. She looked pretty with her red hair all done up in the back, and with long dangling earrings.

Long dangling earrings? Mother hadn't worn earrings since Anneke was really small, before the doctors had diagnosed Mother's schizophrenia.

After a big hug, as they sat side by side in the back of the car, Anneke asked, "Didn't your pierced ears grow shut?"

"I had them redone. Do you like these new earrings?"

"Yes. You look beautiful."

Mother squeezed Anneke's arm lightly. "Thank you. Would you like to have your ears pierced?"

"No, thanks. I don't like wearing jewellery. I'd rather get a new carving tool. Or actually a new CD is what I really need."

"Let's go shopping after breakfast," Mother said. "I got my first pay cheque last Friday. So I want to treat you."

Anneke remembered Mother's new job at the group home, but she wasn't going to let it bother her. She pushed away the little voice that pouted, "I want us to move back together." Instead she listened to another little voice, the one that said, "Breakfast with Mother. Yippee!"

"Are you hungry?" Mother asked. "I am."

"Yes, very. My stomach is still catching up after a

weekend of beans and beans and then more beans."

They ordered big meals of pancakes and mugs of hot chocolate. While they waited for the food to arrive, Anneke set the two netsuke on the table.

Mother gasped as she picked one up. "These are beautiful," she said. "Did you carve...no."

"I found them," Anneke said. And then followed the long story of her and Ken's and Sheera's adventures.

When there were no more details to tell, when they'd mopped up the last of the sweet syrup with the last bites of pancake and drunk the last drop of hot chocolate, Mother said, "Larry phoned last night. He talked to Dr. Sunnybrook. Then Dr. Sunnybrook talked with me this morning. She told me that I need to explain better why I am staying at the group home."

A little voice crashed its way into Anneke's head and she said, "Your schizophrenia is better now. I waited for such a long time to move back with you."

"I know," Mother agreed. "Explaining things about me is hard. But I promised Dr. Sunnybrook that I would try my very best."

Anneke, her bossy voice taking over, said, "I want you to rent a place. We'll live together again, you, me, and Sheera. Like we used to."

Mother shook her head. "Right now I'm doing really well. Dr. Sunnybrook agrees. But she says that with schizophrenia you never know. I still have voices that tell me to do things. Dr. Sunnybrook says that we can't live together. Not until you are an adult." Mother's hands had rested on either side of her plate. Now she reached across to Anneke.

"Dr. Sunnybrook, Dr. Sunnybrook! I hate her! What does she know?" Anneke kicked the big metal leg in the middle of the table. She was only wearing sandals, and her toe hurt. Even so, she kicked the table again.

Mother lightly squeezed Anneke's hands. "She knows. She's very good to me. I'm lucky to be her patient. I have so much going on in my head, and she helps me a lot."

"She's not *us*," Anneke whispered. "How does she know?"

Mother's hands started shaking. She let go of Anneke, balled her hands into fists, and squeezed her eyes shut. One tear dropped from a lid and slowly slithered down her cheek. "I have to try harder," she whispered.

After a short silence she said, "Remember, Kindeke, you just told me about the mother bear and the collar? So they can keep checking her out?" A tear slipped slowly down the other cheek.

Anneke put her hands on Mother's fists. "But we're people," she said.

"I know," Mother went on, opening her fists and taking Anneke's hands again. "Dr. Sunnybrook will make sure everybody is safe. She said we don't need to hurry into anything." Mother let go of Anneke's hands and dried her cheeks. "Just think how lucky that cub is to have a new mother bear to teach her things."

Anneke wished she'd called the cub Unlucky. But then again, the cub *was* lucky.

"I will always love you more than anyone," Mother said. "Always. No matter what, you will always be my daughter. But Eileen loves you too. So does Larry. Can you try to love more than one adult at the same time?"

"I do, but..." Anneke shook her head. She couldn't think. Her head was too full of little voices. Voices talking to her all at once. Confused, she whispered, "I hear voices too. They tell me I should live with you. Sometimes I wonder if I have schizophrenia."

Mother smiled and took her daughter's hands again. "No, Kindeke. Everyone has voices in their heads that say 'Yes, do this. No, do that.' They argue, they convince, they make you feel excited or happy or sad. Dr. Sunnybrook says that's normal. Those voices are only thoughts. But my voices are different; to me they are real people. People who have real bodies and real names. I hear them. I see them. I talk out loud to them. They are a big part of my life. They answer me. They tell me what I should do. How I should live. Where I should go. Sometimes they tell me to do bad or scary things."

Anneke looked puzzled. "And nobody *is* really there?"

"Right," Mother said. "Dr. Sunnybrook explained it all to me. She is helping me to see that there is nobody around when I think there is. That sometimes I am delusional."

"I don't mind," Anneke said.

Mother sighed and said, "I can't give you what you need."

"Yes, you can," Anneke cried out.

Briefly Mother squeezed her eyes shut, but then, resolutely, she said, "No. You have so much talent. You could be a famous artist one day. I believe that. Larry and Eileen believe that. Everyone who has seen your carvings thinks so. Dr. Sunnybrook says that you need a good home with opportunities and guidance. I can't give you that, but Larry and Eileen can. You are lucky to have them as a family."

Anneke nodded. "I know. I love them. But it's hard with Eileen sometimes. I don't want them to adopt me. Mostly because I don't want Eileen to be my mother. I like her OK, but I want *you* to be my mother."

"I am. You don't need to be adopted. But be a part of their family. Love us all. In our hearts there's always room for one more to love. So you're lucky. You have two mothers. Some kids don't even have one."

Silently Anneke nodded, feeling Mother's thin hands shaking slightly in her own. Then Mother said, almost shyly, "Someday I'd like to go on a camping trip with you and Larry."

"Yes." Anneke smiled broadly. "I'll tell Larry. I know he'll say yes. He really likes you. Everybody does."

They left the restaurant, and when they passed the bookstore, Mother helped Anneke choose a get-well card and a present for Ken. They decided on a book about wildcats of the Pacific Northwest. Then, walking side by side, they set off again down Baker Street towards the music store.

CHAPTER 15

Anneke had just gotten back from Nelson when Ken phoned to tell her about his broken arm and all his cuts and scratches.

"I hope you'll be OK soon," she said. A little tensely she asked, "How's your mom?"

"Fine. But I'm not allowed on the computer for two weeks. And I'm not allowed to play with you for the rest of July." His voice became a whisper. "At first she had a hairy fit. But now a man called Mr. Onoda is coming over for tea this afternoon. She's all excited. The guy who helped me, Mr. Richards, told us that Mr. Onoda had three netsuke stolen from his place. So my mom thinks that he *may* be related to us, because of the netsuke. And my mom wants you and Larry to come over for tea. And bring the netsuke."

"I'll ask." Anneke didn't particularly want to face Mrs. Uno so soon. But she did want to hear about the carvings. After all, she was the person who had rescued the first one from the river. And found the second one as well. But then, maybe this wasn't a good time to remind anyone of those stunts.

She had barely put the phone down when Mr. Parker called with the promised report. He told Anneke that when the mother bear had first woken up, she'd cuffed Lucky, who was trying to nurse. The sow had chased Lucky up the tree with her other cub. She'd stumbled around, sniffing, slept some more, and had finally called the two cubs down. The last Mr. Parker saw of them, the mother was showing both cubs how to claw apart a rotten tree stump to eat all the ants.

Anneke felt herself grinning as she handed the phone to Larry. In the hallway she ran into Eileen. "The mother bear adopted Lucky," she said. "Mr. Parker told me that I saved the cub's life."

"Great," Eileen said. "I'm sure the mother bear is happy to have two cubs again instead of one."

"I think so. But for Lucky, her real mother isn't around anymore."

Eileen looked at her. "But yours is. And I don't want to replace your mother." She opened her arms and Anneke walked into them.

"You know," Eileen said, "all we wanted to do was let you know how much we want you here. You really are a part of our family."

After a big hug, Anneke rushed to her workshop, an idea for an abstract carving forming at the edges of her mind—a design to whittle out of an especially beautiful chunk of cherrywood Larry had given her last spring. She picked up the wood and turned it slowly, lovingly in her hands. She could see the colours, could already imagine its beauty: a smooth, shiny form with long, slender shoots, like strands of ivy, weaving in and out of each other. The shoots would be like arms, hugging arms, intertwining. Not just two arms, or four, but many. Too many to count. They would all weave in and out, over, under, and through each other, without a beginning or an ending. She'd have the carving finished by the time the baby was born. It would be her goddess of family. She would polish the cherrywood to a real shine. And this carving would never be for sale. Never!

Later that afternoon, as they drove into the Unos' driveway, Larry reminded Anneke to be on her best behaviour.

"Don't worry!" she said. "I will! It's a promise I'm keeping, too. You're wearing your good hiking shorts and belt again."

"So are you," Larry grinned. "Who says we can't be twins, like we were at the Fathers and Daughters camp?"

First Anneke made a face at Larry. But then, finally, as easily as hot beans sliding off a stick, the words slid from her lips. "Thanks, Dad."

Larry parked the truck, squeezed her shoulder, and said, "You're quite a daughter to have, you know."

Anneke grinned. "I know." Quickly she hopped out of the truck. Walking to the front door, she slowed her pace more and more, not knowing what she should say or do when the door opened. All she knew was that she'd be on her very best behaviour.

Ken opened the door. He held out his cast and a felt pen. "Sign it," he demanded.

In memory of your first camping night Anneke wrote. She added her own and Sheera's names.

"I'm sorry about everything," she mumbled.

"Sure," he said. "Guess what." A smile spread across his face. "Darryl bought this cool, new, big-screen TV and some DVDs about animals. He's going to invite me over to watch them."

"And guess what," Anneke said. "My mom is coming camping some time. Maybe she can borrow your mom's tent and stuff."

"Sure. I don't think my mom will want to use it for a long time."

They walked into the living room, where Mrs. Uno was busy pouring Larry a cup of tea. One good thing about coming here, Anneke thought, looking at the table. Mrs. Uno always had lots of fancy cookies. And she was very generous with them. Although, Anneke decided, since she was on her best behaviour, she'd only have one cookie. Well, maybe two. Absolutely no more than three!

Mrs. Uno introduced a man already sitting in the living room as Mr. Onoda. He had short, short black hair and a smile as friendly as...As friendly as Ken's smile. Anneke looked from one to the other.

While Mrs. Uno poured the kids glasses of lemonade, Anneke gave Ken his card and book. Then she put her two netsuke on the table beside Mrs. Uno's.

Mr. Onoda took them and nodded. "These are the missing ones," he said. He smiled at Anneke from ear to ear.

"First, let's get to the bottom of where these netsuke came from," Larry said, suddenly looking serious.

"Ken told me about how you two found this little guy, Hotei, in the river," Mr. Onoda started.

Anneke threw her friend a thankful look while he held out the cookie plate to her. She took only one, the one with the most chocolate.

"And this netsuke that you found at the cabin," Mr. Onoda continued, "is Daikoku, the god of warriors and wealth."

Mrs. Uno added, "The one Mr. Richards found in the cabin is Fukurokuju, the god of wisdom and a long, lucky life."

"So now, between the two families, we have the whole set," Ken said.

Mr. Onoda picked up the two gods Anneke had found and said, "I had three netsuke. My parents gave them to me many years ago. One day someone broke into my house and stole a lot of my things. The police later returned some of my stolen property but never these three netsuke. How Hotei ended up in the river is a mystery to me. Maybe the thief lost the carving when he ran off to that cabin in the woods. He must not have known that they are valuable antiques or he would have looked after them better."

Mrs. Uno said, "The amazing part is that, through them, we found each other." She looked at Mr. Onoda.

"Yes," he said, lovingly stroking Hotei's shining head. "Our grandparents," he pointed at Mrs. Uno and himself, "would have been so happy to know that I found you again."

"So you are definitely related to us?" Ken asked.

"Yes, very distantly," Mr. Onoda smiled. "I'm sort of like a distant uncle, you could say. Uncle Toshi. Toshihiro is my first name."

"Cool," Ken said.

"And," Uncle Toshi said, putting Hotei back on the table, "it all started when Anneke rescued this netsuke from the river."

Anneke looked at Larry, then at Hotei.

"These are happy-looking little gods," Larry said. "They look like I feel."

"I have my netsuke back," Uncle Toshi said. "And, more importantly, my long-lost relatives. Thanks to you, Anneke. I'd like to repay you. How about a fishing trip on Slocan Lake in my new, fast boat for you and Ken. If you are allowed, of course."

"Not right now," Mrs. Uno said. "Not until Ken's arm is better."

"Oh, he'll be fine," Uncle Toshi said. "I promise we won't throw him overboard and fish for him."

Larry laughed. "This is the one you really have to watch," he said, ruffling Anneke's hair. "She's the one who goes overboard on adventures."

"So that means I can go?" Anneke asked.

"Only if Ken is allowed," Larry said. "And if you keep your promises."

"I guess Ken can go for an hour or so," Mrs. Uno said. "Next month. We'll wrap his arm up carefully."

"Oh, Mom," Ken groaned. But when he saw his mother's face darken, he quickly added, "Thanks, Mom."

Just then the cookie plate was passed around again. "No, thank you," Anneke said politely, her mouth watering.

Larry grinned and winked at her. Anneke smiled sweetly, then kicked Ken back under the table.

"We'll take my new book and card upstairs, OK, Mom?" he said.

"We're going home soon," Larry answered. "I'll call you down."

After Ken closed the dining-room door behind them, on their way through the kitchen, he grabbed the cookie jar and held it out to Anneke. She took two double chocolate cookies. And then one more, because she was celebrating.